THE KILL FEVER

SAM RAVEN
BOOK FIVE

BRIAN DRAKE

**ROUGH
EDGES
PRESS**

Rough Edges Press
An Imprint of Wolfpack Publishing
1707 E. Diana Street
Tampa, FL 33610

roughedgespress.com

Paperback ISBN 978-1-68549-452-0
Ebook ISBN 978-1-68549-451-3

THE KILL FEVER

THE CHILLY WIND COOLED THE NERVOUS SWEAT ON MEGAN'S face. She'd left the windows of the Audi down and the wind tossed her hair as she drove. One final turn and the target house appeared, hidden within a walled perimeter, dark except for front security lights.

Inside, her ticket to a new life.

If she didn't get killed first.

She eyed the back of the property as she approached. Beyond was the Balearic Sea off the coast of Spain. The house's owner didn't spend much time looking at the ocean. Megan knew the occupant directed her attention east to the Barcelona Airport. The owner liked to sit on her east-facing balcony and watch airliners come and go. The jets passed over the house.

Megan pulled over and stopped the car. She toggled the Bluetooth and electronic ringing filled the car. The line clicked but nobody spoke. She knew somebody was on the other end because he was breathing.

"I'm waiting, Charlie," she stated.

The nervous male on the other end rushed his reply.

"The gate is open. Hurry!"

"We have all night, Charlie." Megan pressed End and drove the final twenty yards. The gate wasn't open. It was instead ajar, with a motor behind the wall making a grinding sound. The automatic mechanism had jammed. Megan hopped out, pushed the gate open, and climbed back into the car. The Audi's engine hummed as she drove through.

Megan had been on the run for more years than she cared to remember. No last name, no family, and no future unless she succeeded tonight. She was one of the millions of Nicolae Ceausescu's street children, born to a family who couldn't afford her, abandoned at birth, and raised in a government orphanage. It had been Ceausescu's idea to outlaw abortion and contraception in Romania in the '60s, his decree that couples have as many children as possible to build up the nation's population. The policy remained in place until his death. The consequences led to a lost generation to which Megan belonged.

While others like her had worked to find a normal life, Megan had turned to crime. Not by choice, but circumstances beyond her control. She'd learned to survive by stealing; now, she targeted people like the owner of the mansion. What she planned to steal tonight would put an end to her struggles forever. A yellow manila envelope containing pictures, pictures the intelligence community of the United States desperately wanted. Every thug and cutthroat were looking for them, too.

But she'd found them first.

The wind blew harder, brushing her neck to give a head-to-toe chill. But she was closer to her goal now more than ever. Between the noise from the wind and the car, she didn't hear the saw buzz sound of the remote drone flying overhead.

TWO MILES AWAY, near a cliff overlooking the Balearic, a man named Augie Buchanan sat inside a gray panel van. Glowing computer monitors shined on his rough face. On the short table in front of him, he operated the controls of the drone flying over the mansion. Each screen displayed what the drone's camera eye saw, either a close, medium, or far shot.

"New arrival at the gate."

The wireless comm link in his right ear transmitted his words to two other men. His teammates were about to climb over the west side wall.

"Say again?"

The voice of Logan Shaw, leader of the three-man team, was soft in Buchanan's ear.

"Black Audi coup. Unknown number of occupants but the driver is female. She pushed open the gate and is halfway to the front door." Buchanan adjusted the drone's position to focus on the mansion's front door. "The front door is opening and a man is stepping onto the porch."

Shaw replied, "Our tip said the house would be empty."

"You're telling me?"

No reply. Buchanan kept the camera focused on the door. He needed to see how many exited the Audi. He needed to know how many they now faced. Their informant had claimed the house would be empty. The entire plan hinged on the incoming information. Shaw and their third man, Tony Webb, would be discussing the development, deciding whether to abort. Buchanan's info would be critical to the final call.

The three men were American mercenaries employed by a tough Croatian named Branko Zupan. Their orders were explicit. Break into the house, loot the safe, and bring back a yellow manila envelope. None of them knew the significance of the envelope or what it contained, but it didn't matter. This kind of raid was their specialty. The envelope was as good as theirs.

"The woman is exiting the car," Buchanan said. He watched a moment longer, added: "She's alone."

"Who is at the door?"

Buchanan examined the close shot. "Looks like the butler. Our intel wasn't accurate, Logan."

"The little snake sold the same information to whoever the woman is," Shaw said. "Stand by, Augie."

"Copy."

Dealing with a two-timing informant wasn't the priority right now, Buchanan knew. They needed the material the mansion's owner had locked in her bedroom safe. He knew what Shaw would decide. Buchanan had worked with Shaw and Webb for fifteen years and felt no hesitation in his prediction. They'd wait for the woman to emerge with the items, then take them from her. No sense breaking a sweat when somebody else did the hard work.

"We wait for her," Shaw said. "Copy, Augie?"

Buchanan grinned. "Copy, wait and ambush."

"Stay in the van," Shaw continued, "and we'll use the Audi to get to you."

"She's inside and the butler has shut the door."

"We're going over the wall."

Buchanan rotated the drone to the western wall. He watched as the heads of Shaw and Webb appeared over the top. "I see you. Grounds are clear."

MEGAN STOPPED the Audi and shoved the gear stick into Park.

She left the car and tugged on her utility belt. A jacket

ending below her hips concealed a tight black outfit and her slender figure. She was tall with long legs and bony fingers; had the gaunt features of somebody who never had enough to eat. She was naturally stoic; her expression often flat, as if she was bored. She climbed the steps. The house butler, Charlie, sucked in a mouthful of air.

"You have a gun," he said.

"Among other tools," Megan said. She pushed him into the house and shut the door.

"But you said—"

"I'm not going to shoot you, Charlie."

The circular entryway contained white marble tile and a row of statues on the forward wall. A spiral staircase curved to the second floor. A hallway to the left led to other parts of the house.

"Our deal stands," she told him. "Forget the gun. Show me the safe."

The butler, in street clothes rather than his usual uniform, shook a little.

"Now!" she commanded.

Megan was a foot shorter than the butler but she didn't hold back the order. Charlie took the lead up the staircase to the second floor. Megan followed. She moved with measured steps, turning her head to take in every angle, watching for threats. Her right hand was never far from her pistol. The gun was a scuffed Beretta 92, and the scuffs came from incidents where survival depended on the messages of death from the gun's muzzle. Her belt contained her safe cracking tools and another handy item, a stun gun. The Taser often took care of distractions like Charlie the Butler.

They reached the second-floor landing and advanced down a dark hallway. The thick carpet muted their footsteps. Only Charlie's heavy breathing disturbed the silence.

The owner was away for two days and had given the staff

both days off. Charlie wasn't a happy employee, and for a cut of the money the envelope brought, he'd agreed to deactivate the property's electronic security system. But he didn't know the combination to the safe. No matter. Megan knew how to solve such problems.

"Walk faster," she snapped.

"Bedroom's here."

Charlie opened a door and stood aside. She gestured for him to enter first. Megan punctuated the silent command by moving her right hand to her gun. The butler stepped into the bedroom.

"Leave the light off."

"Okay."

"Where's the safe?"

"Behind the Queen."

Megan took a small flashlight from her belt and shined the beam where Charlie indicated. The safe was in the wall concealed by an old painting of young Queen Elizabeth. Charlie pulled a corner of the painting and it swung outward on a hinge.

"Thank you, Charlie."

Megan moved her right hand to the left side of her belt, snapping out the Taser. She fired the prongs into Charlie's back. The butler let out a sharp cry as the volts blasted through him. His back arched and he dropped to the carpet, shaking. A swift kick in the side of the head put him out cold.

She put the Taser away. "Sorry, Charlie."

Megan grunted with effort as she dragged his body away from the wall. Why were unconscious men so heavy?

Wiping her hands on her jeans, she addressed the safe. From her belt she donned a stethoscope, fitting the earpieces, and let the end dangle. The simplest tools were always the best, and Megan found the simplicity of her tools better than the fickleness of high-tech equipment. She didn't trust gadgets to crack boxes. Gadgets might fail at a critical moment. Cracking by hand took time, concentration, and patience, but produced the best results, every time. She'd learned all three from a safe cracking expert named Philip. He'd also been her lover. He was gone now and she missed him.

She pushed thoughts of Philip out of her mind and put the end of the scope against the safe door above the combination knob. Listening for the tripping of the tumblers and drive pin was critical.

She had to get the tumblers into position, so the drive pin dropped into the tumbler notches. The effect wouldn't happen until the notches aligned.

She began turning the knob and listening to the inner workings. Three clicks told her the safe combo had three numbers. She'd expected as much with the medium-sized unit but had to make sure before continuing.

She turned the knob back and forth, clockwise and counterclockwise, listening, changing direction each time a tumbler clicked into place. When the third and final tumbler lined up, the drive pin dropped into place with a satisfying *thunk*.

Megan smiled. The thrill never left and she enjoyed the tingling sensation in her spine. She wrecked the door open.

She stared for a moment at the items inside. Only the yellow manila envelope held her complete attention. Inside, her freedom. A new life. The power to make a major world government bend to her every request.

Shedding her jacket, Megan pulled off the pouch strapped to her back and took the envelope from the safe. Opening the flap, she confirmed the set of photos inside, and put the envelope in the pouch and the pouch back on. She donned the jacket again.

Megan closed the safe and returned the tools to her belt.

She swung Queen Elizabeth back to her proper position, winking at the figure in the painting. She left the room without checking on Charlie.

2

LOGAN SHAW AND TONY WEBB LAY FLAT ON EITHER SIDE OF the dormant fountain in the center of the circular driveway. The black Audi coup sat ten yards ahead. They waited for the woman to walk out the front door.

They'd left their safe cracking gear on the other side of the wall. There was no need for the extra weight. Shaw would have preferred having a rifle or carbine, but they hadn't planned on combat. All he had was the Glock-17 in his right hand, the magazine stuffed with 17 rounds of nine-millimeter hollow points. The autoloader would have to suffice. Webb carried the same pistol.

Buchanan's drone continued to buzz over the property until he said, "My battery is low. Gotta call the drone back."

"If she finds another way out, we won't have eyes," Shaw said.

"Can't help it, boss."

"Okay," Shaw said.

The drone's buzz began a slow fade and the night sounds took over. The breeze continued, bringing the chill, and crickets chirped across the yard.

They waited.

She was taking her time, but they'd have their opportunity to grab the bundle and leave her behind soon.

NEVER GO out the way you entered.

One of Philip's mantras, and top of Megan's mind as she prepared to exit. She used her flashlight to find her way to the stairs and descended to the ground floor. The front door was the fastest and easiest way to go, but she cut across the entryway instead. She knew of an exit on the east side of the house.

The flashlight beam led the way through a hallway into an indoor pool. Glass doors on the opposite side opened onto a wide patio. Megan skirted the pool. The room wasn't choked with heat or chlorine; the pool water was still under a full-length cover. She reached the glass doors and flicked the latch.

Cold air blasted through the gap. Megan slipped outside and moved around the patio furniture. A hedgerow divided the concrete and grass. She dropped behind a hedge to watch and wait a few moments. She stowed the flashlight in her jacket.

A chill not from the wind crawled up her back, settled on her neck, and caused her body to shake. The wind carried a voice with it; she wasn't alone. A man's voice, though his entire line of dialogue didn't reach her. She did hear, "Okay..." and then nothing.

And something else. A swarm of bees? She knew the sound well. A drone. The noise receded. Megan knew somebody waited between her and the Audi.

Using the Audi to get away wasn't impossible, but she might have to get creative. Megan crawled around the hedge, across the grass, and blended with the shadows over the lawn. She was glad the house's owner had shut off the rear exterior lighting. She reached the side and stopped at the corner. A peek around the side. The fountain. A shadow beside it didn't match the rest. A man lay there. She pulled away to think.

Questions flooded her mind. Who was waiting? Who else knew about the contents of the safe?

Answers would come later if she still cared. For the moment, she was losing her focus. Over the wall? The nearest part of the wall sat twenty yards to her left. Trees in front would help her climb high enough to swing over the top. She didn't relish the landing. She also wasn't sure if the top of the wall was lined with barbed wire or shards of glass. *Should have checked!* she chided herself.

If she opened fire, they might run. Unless they had guns, too.

Make up your mind, girl.

She couldn't lay on the grass forever.

Megan scooted from the corner and stood. Time to climb a tree and hop over a wall. She wasn't far from city activity. A walk would be nice. A long walk, yeah. *Them's the breaks.* She might find a taxi halfway. She didn't need the Audi; it was a rental, booked via an alias. Nothing in the car connected to her.

She broke into a run. A male voice, the same from moments earlier, yelled, "She's going for the wall!"

Megan ran faster. The wall grew in size as she neared.

Pistol shots cracked behind her.

Megan's heart rate spiked. She screamed as the bullets buzzed around her. Muscles in her back tensed. She expected to feel the punch of a bullet any second. But the shots smacked the grass and whistled over her head. They didn't want to risk destroying the envelope but didn't know how she carried the bundle. They were shooting to knock a leg out from under her.

She dived into the grass, sliding a little, and rolled onto her back. She clawed for the Beretta under the flap of her jacket. Extended the pistol. Two targets. Both male. One used the corner for partial cover. The other squatted in the open. Megan fired, not aiming, the nine-millimeter pistol popping in rapid succession.

The shooter behind the corner shrank out of sight. His partner rolled right--her left. She tracked him and fired twice. Rolling onto her stomach, she jumped to her feet and ran to the wall. The trees swallowed her silhouette. Return fire didn't touch her. One shot chunked into a tree trunk beside her. Another whined off the solid concrete of the wall.

SHAW HADN'T EXPECTED to face another gun.

But the lady had one.

Shaw retreated from the corner of the house as Webb rolled across the grass. Her salvo zipped by them.

Buchanan in his ear. "Need help, boss?"

Shaw fired twice at the tree line. He had no target, but he might get lucky. Nobody screamed down range.

"Bring the van," Shaw said. "She's going over the wall. Won't get far running."

"On my way."

Shaw snapped to Webb, "Cover me, Tony. We fall back to the gate."

Webb kept his Glock aimed at the tree line. "You're covered. Move!"

Shaw ran to the fountain, shouted for Webb, and Webb ran to him while Shaw covered the retreat. No shots fired. The woman had already scaled the wall. They had to move fast, but they had an advantage. Nobody else but her would be on the street this time of night.

Buchanan said, "Thirty seconds out."

"Copy," Shaw said. "Double time!" He and Webb ran the length of the driveway, keeping to the right, and the van screeched to a stop in front of the gate.

Buchanan yelled out the window, "Unlocked!"

Shaw hauled open the side door. Webb jumped inside. Shaw followed. He left the side door open. Buchanan pulled into the street.

MEGAN DIDN'T HOP over the wall.

She stayed on her belly, in the shadows, and watched the shooters retreat. She might be able to get back to her car after all. When the engine of their van rumbled and faded, she knew she had her chance. Easier to escape in a car than on foot. And she wouldn't break her ankle if she botched the landing on the other side.

Philip had always told her to be ready to change plans fast.

Still clutching the Beretta 92, she sprinted across the grass. Her lungs burned, she felt the strain in her legs, but she did not stop. Megan yanked open the driver's door and dropped behind the wheel. She tossed the Beretta on the passenger seat and started the car. The Audi jumped to life.

She turned left after exiting the gate, flooring the gas pedal, and passed a perpendicular road on her left. The opposition's van was midway down the street. As Megan blasted by, she glanced in their direction. The van's brake lights flared red.

3

They had to have seen her in a mirror; at least heard the Audi's revving motor.

Megan faced forward. As she made a right to go south on Ave. Del Mar, the van showed behind her. *Yup.*

Ave. Del Mar ran straight to the coast, then connected to Autovia de Castelldefels. The Autovia traveled east-west. She could go east to the airport and find cover there. The bad guys wouldn't dare open fire. But she had to reach the airport first.

Her eyes darted left and right. Open fields. Farms. Industrial facilities. Most of the structures had no light. The fields were pitch dark. Not the place for a fight. She at least overpowered the van, but the headlamps in the rear mirror seemed to get larger every second. And the Audi wasn't faster than a bullet.

Orange bursts of flame winked from the passenger side of the van. A shot nicked her right mirror, but the others didn't touch the car. The shooting stopped. They weren't close enough and had the same problem she had, limited ammo.

No safe cracker goes to work expecting a gun battle. Megan carried the Beretta to control and deter, not to fight multiple subjects who might out-gun her.

No more of the scenery blazing by caught her eye; she focused ahead. She watched for the connection to the Autovia. Once on the road, she might have enough surrounding traffic to lose the van or get them to back off. They'd for certain break off once she entered the property of the Barcelona airport. Handling them another time might be unavoidable. A delay would give Megan a chance to call for help or at least get more ammo.

The white headlamps behind her drew closer. She frowned. Did they have a supercharger on the engine? She pressed the gas pedal. The lamps fell back, then surged. Yeah. They had something hot under the hood and now they'd be in pistol range and she wasn't anywhere near the Autovia.

The Audi's motor hummed as she kept the speedometer above the limit. Megan controlled her breathing, but her racing heartbeat made staying calm difficult. She thought of Philip. What would he do?

She came up blank. Philip had never covered a situation like the one she now faced.

Wing it, girl.

The van's lights grew larger. Orange flashes on either side sent a jolt of fright through her. With two guns they'd hit her or the car for sure. She'd couldn't go much faster. The Autovia had a left-hook on-ramp. If she took the turn too fast, she'd roll the Audi. If she slowed the enemy would have her. *Dammit! Think!* She started breathing faster. No keeping cool now. She was on the verge of panic.

No! Control yourself!

The back window cracked. She screamed. The bullet continued into the car to *chunk* into the car stereo. *Ha! Wasn't using it anyway.* The air whistled through the hole in the tempered glass.

Two lanes. She had an idea. Megan wrenched the wheel left, reached the opposite lane, and stomped the brake pedal. The Audi's nose dipped and the van shot by. She grabbed for the Beretta and hit the gas again. She stuck the gun out the open window and pulled the trigger. She fired at the back of the van, weaving as the van weaved. Holes sprouted in the rear doors. She fired again and again. One of the back windows broke into pieces. The van veered off the road, rocking as it hit the shoulder. Megan floored the pedal and dropped the Beretta beside her again. She looked back. The van sat off the road, the headlamps shining on open dirt. She smiled and started watching, once again, for the Autovia on-ramp.

Almost there.

THE BACK GLASS CRASHED. Pieces flew into the van but Shaw didn't notice. Buchanan, behind the wheel, screamed. He slapped a hand to the right side of his head. Blood seeped between his fingers and trickled down his neck. He lost control of the van.

"I'm hit!" Buchanan yelled. The van jumped from pavement to dirt. The three men rocked with the jolts as the van rolled over rough ground.

Buchanan slammed the brakes. The van stopped violently. Shaw collided with the dash while Webb smacked into the back of Buchanan's seat.

"Let me see!" Shaw shouted, grabbing for Buchanan's hand. The side of his own face hurt from hitting the dash. He ignored the pain.

Webb shouted, "Let me up front! She's getting away!"

"How bad?" Buchanan asked.

Shaw laughed and dropped back into the passenger seat. "Drive, sissy, she nicked your earlobe."

"Friggin' hurts, man!" Pain vanished from Buchanan's face. He spun the wheel. His bloody right hand slipped. He wiped the hand on his pants. He powered the supercharged van across the dirt to the road.

"Lights ahead!" Webb yelled.

"We got her," Shaw said. "She slowed a little."

"I'll kill her myself," Buchanan said. Blood stuck to his face. More blood flowed from the damaged earlobe.

"Make sure we get the pictures," Shaw said. "The pictures are more important."

Buchanan grunted in reply. The van closed the distance with the Audi ahead.

MEGAN CURSED.

Twin headlamps once again pieced the darkness behind her. The spider-webbed rear glass created a kaleidoscope of the bright circles.

The on-ramp was ahead. She sped up. The van closed in, Megan audibly urging the Audi to reach the ramp. The left-turn connector finally appeared. She turned the wheel, speeding along the length of the ramp to finally merge with the Autovia. Next step, get to the Barcelona Airport. And lose the goons chasing her.

She swung the Audi across to the right lane. There wasn't much traffic, but there were enough cars to make it tough to spot her. In the dark with the lights on, you couldn't tell the make and model of a car till you were close.

Megan hoped she was the only Audi on the road. She didn't want an innocent driver mistaken for her. Would they look for the broken back window? Had they been close enough to know they'd hit the car?

She had to keep her mind on getting to the airport. Never mind the rest. *Get to the safety of the airport.*

4

BUT SHE KEPT LOOKING BACK. FORWARD. BACK. FORWARD. Back. And two bright headlamps merged onto the Autovia from the Ave. Del Mar connector.

Steady, girl.

She felt for her gun and jammed it under her left thigh. How many rounds left in the magazine? Might be five, or one. The gun would become a paperweight when the last shot left the muzzle. She faced three determined opponents. What happened when her gun was empty?

Airport. Stop thinking of anything else.

The lights of the van weaved in and out of lanes, tail-gating other vehicles before veering off to race to the next. Closer. A sign gave notice of the distance to the airport and she made a quick calculation. Five miles to go. She went over a rise in the road and the bright lights of the airport appeared in the distance.

Think of something fast you're not gonna—

The van crowded her back bumper. The headlamps shined into the car. Gunfire cracked. She heard the shots this time. Bullets smacked into what remained of the rear glass and cut into the steel body. Megan swallowed a scream and ducked her head as low as she dared, stepping on the gas. The Audi surged ahead but the van kept pace. Another shot blasted through her driver's side mirror. Megan searched for an exit. Trees lined the road, flashing past as the Audi screamed along. Apartments. Motels. Large buildings looming off the roadway, crowding the space. No exit. The buildings cleared and a sign showed the exit for a beach. Turnoff ahead. She began to make the turn but then a bullet punctured a rear tire.

She fought the wheel as the back end began to slide, then held as the run flat grabbed the road again. Megan turned off at Carrer de Begur. The streetlamps were spaced far apart, casting a light glow. She powered the Audi down the road looking for a place to stop and run.

The van turned behind her.

If she didn't act fast there would be nowhere to go but into the eternal darkness where Philip waited.

IT WAS rare for Sam Raven to be in one place long enough to enjoy a cigar.

He stood in front of the Beach Bar & Grill, a small restaurant catering to the beach crowd. The son of an old friend ran the place. The son had inherited the bar from his late father, and Raven didn't like the kid very much. He was nothing like his old man.

Two apartments sat above the bar. The son lived in one, and often rented out the other. Raven had been staying in the second apartment for the last six weeks.

He was on the run, but not from an enemy. Unless he counted himself as the enemy this time.

Raven puffed on the Padron 7000, savoring the rich

flavor, and tried not to think of what brought him to Spain. The road leading past the bar, Carrer de Begur, was quiet. The only noise came from the ocean far to his right. The crashing waves, this time, didn't bring the solace such an environment usually provided. There was too much on his mind. And no solutions forthcoming.

"Hey, Sam."

A voice from above. Raven turned and looked up. From the open window of the first apartment appeared the head and neck of the bar's proprietor, Sebastian.

"What?" Raven said.

"I don't like tobacco smoke. Put that cigar out."

"I'll put it out when I'm finished."

"Listen—"

"I've been standing here for three quarters of an hour and you're only *now* sticking your generous head out the window?"

"I'm charging you another ten bucks a night, retroactive, for the smoking."

"I'm surprised you know as big as word as *retroactive*."

"Make it twenty."

"You're lucky I admired your father, Sebastian."

The head and neck retreated. The window slammed shut, and peace descended onto Carrer de Begur once again.

But only for a moment.

Raven frowned as the sound of a straining engine broke the silence.

Off to his left. He watched the headlights of a car turning off the Autovia.

Another vehicle, a van, screeched its tires making the turn to follow the car.

"Hello, action," Raven muttered. He drew on the Padron, turned, and blew the smoke toward Sebastian's window. The wind interfered and sent the cloud back in Raven's face. He chuckled.

The oncoming vehicles continued their approach. Two pops joined the racing engines. Raven retreated to the alcove of the bar's entrance. Gunfire. No mistake. Another pop. And the car ahead of the van swung off the road to the left, into the trees, where it stopped. He heard a door open. The van halted behind the car and three men piled out. Raven wished there were more streetlamps, but he saw enough in the available light. The way the three men clutched objects in their hands left no doubt about their intentions. Those objects were guns.

Who were they chasing?

Raven dropped the half-smoked Padron on the ground and hurried inside. He climbed steps in the back of the bar to his apartment.

MEGAN RAN AS FAST as she could.

She breathed in heavy gasps with startled grunts escaping her lips. The uneven ground made every other step a lurch. The trees presented obstacles, too. The darkness prevented her from seeing such obstacles before they threatened to take off her head. Low branches smacked at her. She ran with her body slightly bent, trying to compensate for the changing terrain. And she had no idea where she was going.

She paused at a trunk to look back. Her legs and lungs hurt. She wiped sweat from her face. Her jacket, tool belt, and the satchel across her back added weight she didn't need, but she couldn't shed a single item. Her sweaty right palm held the Beretta 92 but she didn't trust her accuracy in the dark.

The glow of the streetlamps helped a little. The light

made moving silhouettes of the three men chasing her. They ran with ease and confidence. They were in a familiar element while Megan was blind. She was a thief, not a midnight commando.

But as the three men ran deeper into the trees, they'd face the same problem as she. They might navigate the area better, but they'd also have trouble identifying their target. If she could hide long enough for them to pass…

Megan bolted left, the ground sloping. She finally heard the crashing ocean instead of only her hammering heart. She stopped short, skidding a little, as she found a fallen trunk. Megan rolled over the top and dropped flat on the opposite side. She stayed flat with the Beretta at the ready. She still had no idea how many cartridges remained in the gun. Every instinct screamed for her to keep running and she fought back panic. Once the enemy passed, she could get back to the Audi and be gone before they realized she had slipped away.

She wished Philip was with her. He'd know what to do.

They were near. She heard them. One gave orders. He wanted the other two to spread out, create a search pattern. The man's last line chilled her. "She can't have gone very far."

Megan continued breathing hard. They'd hear. She held her breath, but let it out after five seconds. *Slow down, girl.* She forced herself to breathe slower. She hoped the ocean noise covered the sound. If she'd gone a little further it might have.

A twig snapped.

5

Raven left the bar and ran across the street to the Audi. Bullet holes riddled the car. Inside the van, he found the computer equipment, a drone, and monitors.

He left the van and ran into the trees. He gripped his own pistol, a Nighthawk Custom Talon .45 ACP autoloader. He'd screwed a suppressor to the muzzle, but he didn't want to use the gun. Stray bullets might find a way to the Autovia, or one of the apartment buildings lining the beach. He lived by two rules. One, no roots. Nothing to tie him to a single place. Two, no gunfights where innocent people might get hurt. His business was helping victims of predators, not creating new ones.

He ran in a pattern. Straight ahead, a pause to scan his surroundings, then a sweep left. Another pause. A sweep to the right. He listened the entire time for any sounds not part of the natural environment.

Somebody spoke, a man giving orders to two others. The final line, "She can't have gone very far," cemented the situation in Raven's mind. There was a woman on the run. The men chasing her weren't the local police. The van confirmed they were something else.

Raven shifted right again and kept moving, the .45 ready in his right hand.

———————

MEGAN TRIED TO STOP HERSELF. Self-preservation took over, an instinct not sharpened by training or experience. Despite a furious mental battle, she took action anyway.

After the twig snapped, she jumped to her feet, extending the Beretta. As tunnel vision clouded her eyes, she couldn't decide what objects were tree trunks and which was a killer.

Aware of her lack of ammo, she hesitated too long.

A meaty hand grabbed at her wrist and twisted. She cried out as her body turned with the twist and the man yanked the Beretta from her grasp.

"I got her!" the man shouted.

Megan swung, her blows blocked, and a hard object smashed into the side of her head. Her vision spun. Pain exploded in her body. She fought to remain standing. The man held her up. It was the only reason she remained on her feet. His arm was under her right arm and across her chest. He dragged her a few feet away from the fallen tree trunk as he yelled for his compatriots again.

Megan, still woozy, glanced around. Her vision remained blurry, but the outline of another figure appeared. She moaned and tried to break free but the man's iron grip didn't budge.

The new arrival swung his own gun. The man holding her collapsed and she landed on top. She yelled and struggled to get up but only rolled onto her side. She pressed both hands to her head.

Strong hands helped her rise.

"I'm a friend," the new man said. She blinked to stop her spinning vision, but the effort failed. She couldn't overcome the surrounding darkness. Somewhere far away the glow of the streetlamps registered, but they didn't help.

"Stay quiet."

Now she was moving, but not under her own power. Her feet didn't touch the ground. The "friend" carried her and he was hurrying toward the lights.

The only thought Megan mustered was *Where's my gun?*

LOGAN SHAW DROPPED to his knees beside August Buchanan. Tony Webb looked around with his Glock in a two-hand grip.

"Gus?" Shaw examined his teammate.

Webb said, "What's the damage?"

"Blow to the head. Gus?"

Buchanan stirred and groaned.

"Talk to me, Gus."

"Another man," Buchanan muttered. He pointed in the direction Raven and Megan had gone. "He's carrying her."

Shaw rose. "Get him back to the van, Tony."

The team leader didn't wait for a reply. Shaw started running from tree to tree. He needed to find the woman and now whoever else was trying to take her and the envelope from them.

He spotted the figures ahead, their outlines highlighted by the streetlamps. He braced his pistol against a tree trunk and fired once.

RAVEN SWEATED under the strain of carrying the woman, but the bar wasn't far away. His shoes pounded hard on the dirt, crunching twigs, leaves and pine needles. He didn't care about the noise. He had to get the woman away.

A shot cracked behind him.

There was nothing he could do, so he kept moving. The bullet smacked into a trunk to his right.

Another shot whizzed by. Glass shattered in one of the buildings across the street. He lowered Megan to the ground and spun around with the .45 extended. He fired twice, aiming at the shadows, searching for a form not matching the rest. He fired again. Shifting his aim left, he fired twice more. A grunt. He'd scored. Dropping into a crouch, he scanned for a moving shadow, but saw none.

He turned to grab Megan again but she wasn't where he'd left her. She was a few feet away, crawling.

"Come on," Raven said. He grabbed her again and this time hoisted her across his shoulders. She struggled and thrashed but he held tight.

Raven reached the pavement and angled for the bar. The van and Audi were in their spots on the left side of the road about twenty yards away. The van rumbled to life. Raven reached the opposite sidewalk and set the woman down in an alley. He took a knee at the corner and braced the .45 against the wall. The van backed up, turned, and sped away toward the Autovia. He lowered the gun.

The woman finally regained enough strength to bat at Raven, but he hauled her to her feet one last time. He let her lean against him, and finally led her into the bar. He locked the door behind them.

The woman resisted going up the dark stairway. Raven pried her hand from the doorway, muttering assurances. He half-dragged her up the steps. He wouldn't have wanted to go either. For somebody suffering a possible concussion, in the grip of an unfamiliar person, who had survived a murder attempt--yeah, getting hauled up a dark and narrow stairway wasn't going to be high on her list even if none of the other events had taken place.

Entering the apartment was a little better but once again Raven cringed at the sight of the place. The living room was small. Throw rugs on a wooden floor, a couch with thin cushions. Another short hallway to a bedroom with the bathroom sandwiched between. He set her on the couch. She was too long for it, and her legs dangled off the end. But she sighed as she finally rested her head on something soft.

Her jacket fell open. Raven spotted the empty holster and other items on her tool belt. He suspected what the tools were for. While carrying her he'd felt a pack under her jacket. He didn't bother with it now, but noted she shifted several times to get comfortable.

From the bathroom sink, he filled an empty glass with warm water and grabbed a washcloth. He set them on the coffee table in front of the couch. He put a blanket over the woman and dipped the washcloth in the warm water. He started wiping her forehead. She pulled the blanket up and didn't fight him.

"What's your name?" he said. He wiped the sweat from the rest of her face, touched the back of his hand to her cheek. She felt cold. He applied more water to the cloth and wiped her face again.

She breathed hard despite laying down. But she managed to say, "Megan."

"Megan what?"

"Just Megan." She looked at him. He watched her eyes. They spun a little.

She spoke with an Eastern European accent, but it wasn't Russian. Something similar. He'd place it soon enough. "You took a hard blow, Megan." He finally addressed the red welt on the left side of her head. "Stay still, don't do anything strenuous."

THE KILL FEVER | 29

"Are you a doctor?"

"Nope."

"Who are you?"

Raven sat on the coffee table and placed the washcloth on top of the cup.

"I'm Sam Raven."

6

"WELL," SHE SAID, FEELING HER FOREHEAD, "NOW I KNOW WHY you haven't tried to steal my stuff."

"I have enough stuff."

She tried to smile but only groaned.

"I don't know what you're carrying," he told her, "but you can unload it if you like."

"If you only knew," she said.

A knock interrupted them. Sebastian yelled through the door. "Raven!"

Megan attempted to sit up but he told her to stay put. "Minor annoyance," he added. He went to the door and pulled it open.

Sebastian looked mad.

"What the hell is going on? Who is that?"

"A friend."

"You didn't pay for two people."

"Add it to my bill. Retroactive, remember?"

"What happened outside?"

"Never mind."

Sebastian changed from mad to worried. "Did you call the police?"

"Sebastian, please. We both know neither of us are calling the police. I took care of the problem to make sure they didn't come sticking their nose around here, get it?"

Sebastian swallowed.

"You aren't as covert as you think, Sebastian. Your old man was better."

Sebastian scowled and turned back for his room. Raven shut the door.

Megan said, "Who—"

"Don't worry. You need some water, and then rest. I need to move your car, too."

"Back wheel—"

"Shot out, I know. And the window. Is it yours?"

"No."

Megan finally sat up and moved the blanket aside. She removed her jacket, the satchel, and her tool belt and placed them on the coffee table.

"I don't want to know what's in there, do I?" Raven said.

"It's supposed to be a ticket to a new life. Instead, it's a target on my back."

Raven pressed his lips together. He didn't want to pry into her business but understood what she said. He told her to sit tight while he moved the Audi. He went back outside.

She'd left the key fob in the steering column. The Audi wasn't in any ruts. Raven pressed the starter and the engine turned over. He looked back to examine the bullet hole in the back window and then the stereo panel where the bullet had struck. He whistled. She'd been lucky indeed, considering the other bullet strikes on the car. Raven backed onto the pavement. The run flat tire made driving easy, and he steered around the corner of the bar to the rear alley. Nobody would disturb the vehicle, and once the new day began, he'd figure out how to replace the tire. The rest of the damage? No idea. He wasn't sure what to do with the car. Or the woman. Raven had come to Spain to escape his war without end, not find another fight.

He had spent a good part of his life on the front lines, covert or otherwise. 82nd Airborne; Special Forces; CIA Ground Branch; a career serving his country in hostile environments around the globe. A multitude of enemies and brushes with death. He left it behind to settle into civilian life, until tragedy struck, compelling him to take up arms again. Not for his country; not for himself. He fought to keep others from experiencing the tragedy he had. When he failed, he avenged with fire and fury.

The only link to his past was the scuffed sterling silver locket he wore around his neck. He never looked inside. He knew what was there--the ghosts who brought those in need to him. He had hoped Sebastian's rundown apartment might be a good place to hide. But action found him anyway. Megan wasn't the usual type of person to cross his path. If she'd accept his help, he was duty-bound to obey the forces directing him from a higher plane.

But what he wanted more than anything was a long rest. There had been too many recent battles; too many friends lost. He wasn't a machine with the ability to fight forever. But *The Call* kept coming.

He returned to the apartment and found Megan asleep. Raven glanced at her gear and satchel on the table. He wasn't tempted to snoop. He needed to earn her trust and poking through her things would sabotage the goal. He recognized safe cracking tools when he saw them and had plenty of his own. He also knew the attempt on her life was tied to the items she'd stolen.

Locking the apartment door, Raven switched off the

lights and went to the bedroom. He placed his pistol on the nightstand and didn't bother undressing. Megan's "friends" might come back. He wanted to be ready if they did.

MEGAN WAITED for Raven to go to the bedroom and opened her eyes.

Leaving was out of the question in her current state, and she had no idea where he had put the car. She hurt all over. Her head throbbed. The rest of her body didn't feel good either. Best to stay put until healthy function resumed. Or at least until she could walk without feeling dizzy.

She couldn't believe she'd finally come in contact with Sam Raven. She'd never set out to meet him. He wasn't somebody she wanted to meet. His name carried weight in the underworld, and he was loved or hated, no in between. She didn't think he'd look kindly on how she made her living. What would he think when he learned of the circumstances leading to her arrival?

Megan shifted on the couch. The thin cushions weren't terrible. What bothered her was the length, and how her legs dangled at the other end. The curse of being tall and thin.

She considered her present state.

Problem: The stolen envelope. She had to keep the envelope away from Raven. As a former American agent, he'd more likely turn the envelope over to the CIA than let her keep it.

Problem: She didn't feel safe in her wounded state despite Raven and his gun. The enemy knew where she was.

Problem: Goddamn Raven looked good. Talk about getting rescued by the perfect hunk-o-dude. *Stop! This isn't a holiday in Nassau.*

Problem: He reminded her of Philip.

And she wasn't sure how to solve any of the problems. The last one troubled her the most. She lay in the dark and stared at the ceiling for a long time. Finally, she fell asleep for real.

7

LOGAN SHAW DROVE THE VAN. HE FOLLOWED THE SPEED LIMIT heading deeper into Barcelona, and their safe house.

Tony Webb, the team medic, checked out August Buchanan on the floor of the van. With the table and computer gear on one side, there wasn't much room, but Buchanan's wounds weren't horrible.

"Glancing blow," Webb said. "Looks worse than it is. Hurts like hell, right?"

"Imagine your worst hangover," Buchanan said, "and multiply by forty."

"Take it easy a bit."

Shaw said, "Who did we fight back there?"

Webb moved forward, hunching to keep from bumping his head on the roof, to the passenger seat. "The man I'm not sure," he said. "But the woman, I have no doubt, was Megan, the safe cracker."

"Are you sure?"

"Who else? She's the best lone wolf box breaker working the circuit."

"If she works alone—"

"Yeah, yeah, who came to her rescue, I get it," Webb said.

"If she takes off with the pictures, we'll never get them," Shaw said.

"We go back?" Webb said.

"With more guns and ammo than we brought tonight," Shaw said.

He pulled off the Autovia onto city streets.

RAVEN ASKED Megan how she liked her eggs.

"Whatever you're having is fine," she said.

"Cheesy and scrambled," he said.

"Sounds fine. Got any salsa? Mix it in, if you do."

"We can manage salsa, great idea."

They had to raise their voices over the kitchen fan. Raven cracked eggs over the flat-top griddle in the bar's kitchen. The apartment above had no stove, so Raven used the bar facilities before the place opened. It was a little past nine a.m.; the staff didn't show to prepare for the day till 10:30.

Raven dropped six eggs on the griddle and set the shells in a bowl. Megan leaned against a prep counter behind him. As Raven stirred the eggs, she volunteered to grate the cheddar cheese Raven wanted to add. Then she scrounged through a huge refrigerator for the salsa she had suggested.

Megan was moving slow after sleeping well despite the couch and felt like she was on the mend. He wanted to talk about her situation while they ate and hoped she was open to the chat.

Raven stirred the eggs some more once he added the cheese and a tablespoon of salsa. Megan started on the toast and he added several strips of bacon to the cook top.

"Are you always this domestic?" Megan asked.

"Oh, yes," Raven said. "My houseboat doesn't have as large a space as this, but I make the most of what's there."

"Why are you staying here, then? Can't be for the kitchen and the company." She pointed at the ceiling. Sebastian still slept above.

Raven laughed. "No, neither. You could say I'm on the run."

"You're hiding?"

"Yes."

"From whom?"

"Myself," he said. "Problem is, every time I turn around, there I am."

She blinked, and Raven fought back a grin. He didn't think he'd stunned her to silence, but she might need a few moments to process his statement and reply.

He didn't give her time. Scooping the bacon, eggs, and toast onto two plates, he led her to a corner booth. She sat and he put her breakfast in front of her. The flat wooden bench-style seat used a thin mat for padding, and the stuffing had flattened. It didn't make the seat very comfortable.

"I make a mean screwdriver if you can handle one," he said.

"Just the orange juice." She unwrapped her fork and knife from the napkin on the table.

Raven departed and returned with two glasses. Plain OJ for her; he'd sweetened his with a half-shot of Russian Standard.

Raven ate slowly while Megan hurried, taking big mouthfuls, chewing a little, rushing to the next bite. It wasn't hard to guess her background from the behavior. She'd grown up in an environment where if you didn't eat quick you might not get to eat at all.

"I can make more," he said, "if you're super hungry."

She paused mid-bite and a little color drained from her face.

"I didn't mean to embarrass you," he said.

"No. It's an old habit." She drank some juice.

"I understand if you don't feel safe, but you have nothing to fear from me."

"Really?"

"I'll prove it to you." He reached behind his back, under his untucked shirt, and withdrew Megan's Beretta 92. He set the gun beside her plate.

"I went out for it this morning while you were sleeping. It's not clean, but I loaded the mag to capacity, thanks to some nine-mil ammo Sebastian has lying around."

She set down her fork and knife and picked up the gun. Buttoning out the mag, she confirmed the load.

Megan slapped the magazine back into place. "How many shots were left?"

Raven lifted his screwdriver to his lips. "Two." He swallowed a sip.

She shook her head. "They'd have killed me if it hadn't been for you." Megan returned to eating, slower than before. The Beretta lay forgotten beside the plate.

"Was it business or personal?"

"Business. I got a tip on something and I guess they got the same tip."

"Tight window, correct? Last night or not at all?"

"Yes."

"What did you take?"

"Not telling."

"You said it was important enough to give you a new life, or something, right?"

"It is," she said.

"And you won't tell me because—"

"You'll take it."

"If I wanted to, I could have. Last night. Early this morning. What did I do instead?"

She chewed a piece of bacon. "You reloaded my gun."

"And I put the spare wheel on your car."

She dropped her eyes from his and pushed eggs around with her fork. Gooey cheese held clumps of the scrambled eggs together; the red salsa added contrast.

"You're free to go," Raven said, "anytime you want. But if you want my help, I'm available."

8

Megan said, "Thank you and I appreciate everything, but I need to keep my secrets."

Raven shrugged. "Fair enough. No more about what you stole. Now, do you want my help with the other matter? The men who tried to kill you?"

"All I need is help getting out of Spain. I had a safe house lined up, and a boat to get out of the country. I still have time to catch my ride tomorrow morning if you can get me to the safe house."

"You feeling up to a boat ride?"

"If I stay down today, I'll manage. Might be hell but I'm running for my life, right?"

Raven used a half-eaten piece of toast to scoop up the final remains from his plate. He ate it and considered her words while he chewed.

"All right. You'll have an armed escort to your getaway. After that, *au revoir.*"

"What do you want in return?"

"Nothing. You've given me a chance to forget myself for a while. It's payment enough."

RAVEN CHANGED the sheets on his bed so Megan could rest in the bedroom. Her morning shower had been refreshing. Raven ran her clothes through the washer and dryer and she wore his bathrobe while waiting. She didn't leave the apartment. It might have been nice to sit outside, but she didn't want anybody to see her in her "work outfit". She settled for opening the bedroom window and listening to the ocean. The sounds of beach goers punctuated the ocean waves.

Climbing the steps back to the apartment had made her dizzy again. The welt on the side of her head remained ripe, and another reason to stay indoors. Moving about only at night wasn't a bad idea.

She didn't mind resting and dozing. It didn't hurt to stay still and calm down a bit, but she never relaxed. She had bursts of rapid heartbeats now and then as fight or flight took over, even in the most serene moments. She was always moving, like a hungry shark, from one theft to another, one temporary shelter to the next.

She'd been on the run her entire life in one way or another. There was no reason to stop now, and Megan wasn't sure she could anyway. Once she cashed in on the pictures in the envelope, and started her new life with her new face, things would change.

She didn't expect to undo 30 years of mental programming by only changing her face, but it was worth a try.

Megan stretched out on Raven's bed and fell asleep. She slept well, until the dream.

Always the same dream when it happened, which was often.

The young girl she held in both arms sobbed. Megan tried to calm her as she ran along a dark street. Carrying the child meant not running fast, and her heavy breathing added to the exertion. The street was empty. Across the blacktop waited the steps to the neighborhood church. Father Ryan could help the child. Father Ryan always knew what to do.

Her legs strained as she climbed the steps. Megan pushed through one of the heavy oak doors and entered but stopped short in the entryway. Still breathing hard, she set the child on the floor. The girl clung to Megan's left leg. If the girl noticed the condition of the sanctuary ahead, she offered no indication.

The stained-glass windows, shattered, only showed jagged holes in their frames.

Pews smashed in half, overturned. Debris littered the floor.

The cross lay on the floor of the altar, the wood and Christ's body in several large pieces.

Megan covered her mouth with her hands. She no longer felt the child's crushing grip on her leg. Worse, there was no sign of Father Ryan or anybody else. Megan reached for the girl's hand as she advanced into the mess. She yelled for Father Ryan.

Megan and the girl navigated the broken pews, heading left toward the confessional. Father Ryan appeared from around the corner.

"What happened?" the priest asked, squatting before the crying child.

"She's hurt. We need help."

"Seems all right to me."

"What happened to the church, Father?"

The priest stood. "We'll clean it up. Only a little messy."

"You call this—"

Pounding at the front door. Megan pivoted. With each solid slam against the oak, the doors crashed inward. Faceless men swarmed inside.

"Take the child, Megan," Father Ryan said, "and run!"

Megan didn't argue. Scooping up the girl, Megan ran past the unmoving priest, down the hall, another door at the end offering an exit. Her heart raced; she ignored the ache in her lungs. At least the girl had finally stopped crying.

As she reached the door, more pounding on the opposite side stopped her cold. The pounding joined the yelling from the front. There was no way out. No escape from what waited outside…

Megan jerked awake with a sharp gasp. Rolling onto her side, she waited to catch her breath and for the panic to stop. She wanted to run. Her mind raced with questions.

I don't know where I am oh my God where am I?

What's that noise?

She jerked her heard to the open window. Nighttime outside. Ocean waves crashed on the beach in the distance. The sounds reached her panicked state as lucidity returned. She remembered where she was and how she arrived.

Her breathing slowed but her rapid heartbeat continued.

She was not safe. Nowhere was safe. The safe places had been destroyed, yet no one saw the destruction for what it was. She had to run away. Her only hope was to keep running. No more thinking. *Go! Now!*

Megan swung her legs over the bed and hurried to the bathroom between the bedroom and living room. Raven slept on the couch. Had she truly been asleep since breakfast? Her head hurt but Megan ignored the discomfort. At the sink, she splashed cold water on her sweaty face. She rinsed her mouth with Raven's mouthwash. All she needed was her gun, car keys and gear, and all were in the bedroom in a corner where she supposed Raven placed them. Gun still loaded. Envelope undisturbed. She jammed the gun in her pack, took car keys in hand, and slung the pack over her right shoulder.

Megan slipped out of the apartment and exited the bar.

She left the front door open and didn't care if an alarm sounded. In the alley behind the bar, she found the Audi with the spare tire attached as Raven had said. The engine fired with a press of the starter and she reversed out of the alley and onto the street.

She turned onto the Autovia again and picked up speed to match traffic. It wasn't so late she couldn't find a hotel. Her escape plan from the area was still valid. She didn't need Raven. Making a deal with him had been a mistake. Lapse in judgment. Her subconscious knew better and reminded her via the dream.

In real life, there had been no crying child. She had been alone. Father Ryan had been there, and somebody had come through the front doors. And despite Father Ryan's plea, she'd stood in front of the altar and shot dead the new arrival before he killed her.

Part of Megan hated running out on Raven. He had been kind to her.

She hoped he'd understand.

9

BUCHANAN PARKED THE VAN. THEY WERE ONE DOOR DOWN
from the bar, close enough to the alley between the bar and
its neighbor to cut off escape from the alley should their
quarry slip away. Shaw and Webb exited first. Buchanan
followed, pressing a button on the key fob. The motorized
side door whispered shut with a soft click.

Shaw made their mission priority clear. "Kill them both,
get the envelope." They knew they faced at least two opponents, but had the woman and her boyfriend called for back-
up? Shaw and his team assumed there might be more, and
they were ready. Shaw and Webb carried suppressed pistols.
Buchanan held the heavy artillery, a Heckler & Koch MP-7.

Webb reached the door first. He frowned when he saw
somebody had left it open. Shaw gestured for him to go
forward. Webb pushed the door open. He and Shaw entered
and moved to one side. Buchanan entered with the MP-7 at
the ready. He joined Webb on the left side of the doorway.
The bar was empty and dark except for the glow of night
lighting from the corners of the room. Chairs stacked on
tables; the bar clear of any clutter. The three men breathed

slowly as they adjusted to the low light. Buchanan swallowed. His throat felt dry, but his pulse beat normally. The three mercenaries fanned out. Shaw took point with his Glock nine-millimeter pistol in both hands. Buchanan stayed in the rear with Webb in the center.

They expected the targets to be in the second-floor lofts. Shaw found the doorway to the stairwell. It wasn't locked. Buchanan grinned. Somebody was watching out for them. They'd hit so fast the targets wouldn't know what happened. The contents of the envelope were as good as theirs.

SEBASTIAN, the bar's owner, awoke to a low-pitched beep. The door alarm. He had a box on the nightstand plugged into the system to alert him of a breach. He rolled over and switched off the alarm. Rising, jamming his feet into slippers, he walked out leaving a robe behind. He knew he'd locked the door before going to bed as part of his closing routine. He never altered the steps to shutting down for the night. If he had forgotten to shut the door, the alarm would have been beeping for hours.

Was Raven out for a smoke? Sebastian dismissed the idea. Raven knew about the alarm and would have deactivated the system.

Sebastian flicked on the hallway light and the light to the stairwell. He started down the steps but froze in his tracks midway down. Three men with guns blocked his path.

Sebastian almost slipped as he bolted back up to the hallway, yelling Raven's name.

"Sam!"

Gunfire spat behind him. Sebastian flinched as pieces of sheetrock pelted his left cheek. He ran. His legs felt like lead and no amount of effort increased his speed.

He could scream though.

"Sam!"

He reached Raven's door as Raven flung it open. Raven held his own pistol. He raised the gun, using his left arm to sweep Sebastian out of the way. "Inside, get down!" Raven tightened his finger on the trigger but the enemy fired first. A stutter from the H&K submachine gun cut Sebastian down. He fell at Raven's feet.

———

POOR BASTARD DIDN'T HAVE a chance.

The gunman with the MP-7 shouldered the weapon. His partners hugged the wall on either side to get out of his way. The H&K bucked as the man fired.

Raven had no doubt whom he faced. The bright hallway light showed the faces of the enemy in full detail. They were the men who had chased Megan. No mistake.

The salvo of MP-7 slugs ripped into Sebastian's back, shoving him away from Raven. The shocked expression on the bar owner's face lasted only a second. He was dead before he fell at Raven's feet.

Raven fired back. The Talon spit one tongue of flame. The face of the man with the MP-7 caved under the impact of the 230-grain hollow-point. The bullet tore a larger hole out of the back of his head. He dropped, but his partners didn't look back. Their own gun muzzles trained on Raven's face. He let two more rounds go before ducking into his room. Suppressed return fire ripped into the doorway.

Raven ran to the bedroom. Megan wasn't there. He didn't have time to think about her absence. From the closet he grabbed his bug out bag and extracted a smoke grenade from a side pouch. Raven pulled the pin and rolled the canister into the living room. The canister popped and filled the room with thick white smoke.

Raven ran into the smoke. He fired twice in the direction of the door and cut left. He covered his mouth and nose with his left hand, but the smoke stung his eyes. In another two seconds, it didn't matter. He raised a window and jumped.

He didn't fall far. A storage unit below the window, built into the side of the building, lay below. The roof was level with the first floor. The shock of the landing sent a jolt of pain up the length of both legs, but Raven pressed on. Another jump onto the side alley concrete, a second hard landing. And then he ran. His own car waited a block away in the public parking lot used by beach visitors. As he gained the sidewalk where the enemy's van sat curbside, he stole a glance over his shoulder. The remaining two gunners exited through the front and onto the sidewalk.

Raven pivoted, firing once. He sucked air as he fell over backwards. He'd hit a raised crack in the sidewalk, and his bug out bag took the worst of the impact. He rolled into the street, crushing his bag under him every time he rolled over. The van provided cover as he rose. Raven fired once at the hood of the van as a gunner appeared around the front fender. The smack of the slug striking the fender drove the killer back.

Raven swung his aim to the rear, anticipating the second shooter. He'd need to reload soon. He jogged back toward the trees at the same time. Bright headlamps shined on him as another car screeched to a stop. The driver swung the car perpendicular, driver's side facing him, and Megan sat behind the wheel. She thrust her Beretta out the window.

Raven ran around the back of the Audi as Megan started shooting. He hauled open the back door, threw himself inside, and shouted, "Go!"

Megan spun the car around and sped off toward the

Autovia. Raven, on his knees in the back, watched for pursuit.

"They aren't coming," she said.

"How do you know?"

"I shot out two tires."

"Nice," Raven said. He removed his pack and sat forward. Megan took the turn onto the motorway.

"Better buckle up, Raven."

"Did you get out before the shooting started?" Raven snapped his seat belt into place.

"Way before," she said.

"What do you mean?"

She told him.

"Why?" he said.

"It wasn't safe."

"Then why did you come back?"

"It wasn't safe for you, either."

10

RAVEN DIDN'T UNDERSTAND AND TOLD HER SO.

"Stop asking, Raven. I don't know the answers right now. You remind me of somebody who saved me once. I didn't want to go back but I did, okay?"

"You were too late for Sebastian."

"What?"

"He died because you left the fucking *door* open, Megan."

She answered with silence.

"Nothing we can do now," he said. He slapped a full mag into the .45. He didn't want to face more trouble with an almost-empty gun. "Where are we going?"

No answer. She kept her eyes on the road ahead, hands tight on the wheel.

"Answer me, goddammit!"

"Stop yelling!"

"Tell me where we are going. Now!"

"Safe house. The one I told you about."

Raven wished he was up front. With his lips pressed together, fury in his eyes, he stared at the back of her head.

"I don't believe you for one second," he said, "you came back for sentimental reasons."

"It's true."

"What's the other reason?"

Silence. The Audi sped along with the traffic. City lights grew in the distance.

"The other reason, Megan."

"I looked inside the envelope."

"So what?"

"I finally saw what I have, that's what."

"Start explaining."

"Pictures of the American president. He's in a compromising position with the vice-president."

Raven wanted to laugh. "You're kidding."

"I'm going to use them to start my life over. It's the score every thief dreams of, Raven. Once the American government knows I have them, they'll give me whatever I want."

"Where did you steal them from?"

"Some rich big shot's house. I don't know how she got them. Somebody gave me the tip and must have tipped the other crew too."

"Marvelous."

"Now you know."

"You aren't somebody who asks for help, Megan. What do you want?"

"To honor our original deal."

"We left two alive back at the bar. They won't stop. Others will get involved, too. What you're carrying will have every government and pirate looking for you."

"You're right."

"Mrs. Raven didn't raise an idiot. What more do you want that isn't part of our original conversation?"

"Help. I don't normally ask, it's true, but I'm asking you for help."

Now it was Raven's turn to remain silent. Sebastian was dead because of her. He could snap her neck, get the pictures, and call it a day.

But he also had to learn more. Who took the pictures? How did they get out in the wild? Who wanted to use them to undermine the United States? Raven had no love for the current commander-in-chief or his ludicrous female counterpart. But it wasn't in his nature to let the USA sit under a sword of Damocles, either.

He needed the pictures for a different reason, and Megan had them. He had to determine a course of action to get them from her and find their source. Not necessarily in such order.

"Okay, it's a deal," he said. "Where is your safe house?"

"On the coast. We'll be there in another half hour."

Raven shifted in his seat. Might as well stay comfortable. But he held onto his gun.

MEGAN'S safe house was also near a beach, albeit on the opposite side of Barcelona from where they'd come. Far enough from the enemy for Raven to consider the location indeed safe. But only for the time being.

The house was a two-bedroom cottage on top of a rise with a foot path leading to the sand. It was too dark to take in the surrounding scenery. The ocean was audible, the air thick with moisture.

Raven tucked the .45 into his belt and followed Megan inside. Modest furnishings occupied the front room, and very new furnishings, too.

"It's an AirBNB," Megan said. "Here's the other bedroom. You can put your stuff in there."

The bedroom was off a short hallway on the left.

Midway down, on the right, was a bathroom. Master bedroom at the end. She turned on all the lights to show him the kitchen and dining area. All spotless. *All lifeless*, Raven thought. It was a model home for display, not a place one made a permanent domicile. Of course, he chided himself, it was a rental and served its purpose. But part of him, lately, longed for roots and attachments. The more his activities reminded of his solitary life, the more aggravated he felt.

And part of his aggravation stemmed from the subconscious need to ditch the two rules he lived by. No roots. Nothing to tie him down. No gunfights in public. He didn't want to endanger those not involved in his war without end. The conflict around abandoning rule one, which he had more than a single reason to adhere to, bothered him. His last attempt at putting down roots hadn't ended well. Rule two he'd never compromise, but he wanted to live without the need for a gun.

"How are we fixed for food?" Raven asked.

"I put eggs in the fridge. There's coffee. Instant, by the way. Nothing fancy. I wasn't supposed to stay long."

"Let's try and get some rest and we'll sort this in the morning."

"It is morning."

"Then when the sun comes up."

She agreed. Raven returned to the guest bedroom and shut the door. He heard her in the kitchen but tuned out the activity. For a few minutes, he unpacked his bag and set his clothes out for the coming day. Reloading the spent magazine for the .45, he placed the gun and loaded mag on the nightstand. It felt good to climb into bed. The sheets were soft and the blanket and comforter warm. But random thoughts troubled Raven's mind, and sleep eluded him. He reviewed his reasons for getting involved with Megan's scheme and added one more. He wanted to avenge poor Sebastian.

MEGAN SIGHED as she pulled the covers over her naked body. She was finally out of her old clothes. Her skin felt dirty, itchy, despite the use of Raven's shower at the bar apartment. Tomorrow she'd start fresh.

She curled up on her side wishing she had a white noise machine, something to distract her thoughts. Raven was in the other room. She felt attracted to him, which would only help her pull a seduction act if it meant keeping him on her side. Until she didn't need him anymore. She wondered if he had an ulterior motive. How much did he blame her for Sebastian's death, truly? She hadn't meant to get anybody killed, but in her haste to leave, she'd set the circumstances in motion.

She hated thinking of him in such a way. He'd helped her and asked nothing in return. He was more like Philip than she wanted to believe, and thoughts of her late lover made her burst into tears. She was betraying him with thoughts of Raven. If only Philip had been with her...

Maybe, in an odd coincidence of life, he was. In a different form.

RAVEN HEARD Megan crying and felt sad for her. What a night for them both. And he knew she had much more on her mind than she spoke about.

He didn't think she was weak. Raven remembered crying in the dark, too. Many times.

He finally dozed off.

11

LUCKILY RAVEN HAD STORED A ZIPLOC BAG OF TEA IN THE BUG out bag. He'd rather have his fingernails pulled out with rusty pliers than drink coffee. But he didn't say so to Megan. Coffee fanatics could be a sensitive lot. She served breakfast at the dining table. Raven had a look at the beach through the dining room's circular wrap-around window. Blue sky met blue water and white sand. The view cleared his mind after the violence a few hours earlier.

Megan served eggs scrambled with a dab of butter, and pre-cooked ham steaks she microwaved. The ham had popped while in the microwave, and while it was hot, it also leaked water. But it tasted good and Raven didn't complain.

"Tell me more about these pictures," he said. "How did you hear about them?"

She spoke between small bites. Raven noticed she slowed her eating as well, but it looked as if she had to concentrate to do so.

"Whispers in the stream to start. Rumors. I checked around. With others in the circuit, you know. People like me."

"Uh-huh."

"The CIA had people looking hard for something, so I figured the rumors were true. An informer told me who had the pictures."

"And you expect these pictures to be your ticket to a new life?"

"Yes. I'm going to change my face, identity, all of it. Megan will disappear. She was never wanted anyway."

Raven let the comment pass. "Who will you be next?"

"I haven't decided."

"Why change your face?"

"I want to change who I am. The next time I look in the mirror, I don't want to see my face. I want a fresh start."

Raven frowned. Her accent. No last name. A change of face. He figured out where she was from, and it made sense why she wanted a change. "You're one of Romania's orphans, aren't you?"

She looked down at her plate. "Yes."

"I've met others," he said. "But none wanted to make as drastic a change as you're talking about."

Raven knew all about Ceausescu's order for families in Romania to have as many children as possible. But a lot of those families couldn't afford the extra mouths. The resulting tidal wave of homeless children forced the government to become their parents. Two generations of children, now adults, had no family, no real upbringing. They'd lived under awful conditions and abuses. They'd wear the scars till they died.

"You have no idea," she said, "what it's like living with a past like mine."

"I might," Raven said. He watched her over the brim of the mug as he sipped his tea. He didn't elaborate and she didn't press. They didn't have the same scars, but pain is pain. They at least had something in common. They ate some more.

"You were saying about the pictures?" Raven prompted.

"An informant told me who had them."

"A big shot, you said. Got a name?"

"A British woman named Ana Gray."

Raven set down his fork and knife and laughed.

"What's funny?"

He wiped his mouth with a paper napkin.

"I know her," he said.

"Really?"

"Calling her a big shot doesn't do her justice. She's a British upper-class icon. Charities, foundations, old, old money. Three generations of old money. You have no idea who you ripped off."

"You make it sound—"

"Exactly. She uses the public persona to cover private activity. Ana runs a small spy operation on the side. She collects people and information and sells to interested parties."

"You think she found the pictures for the CIA?"

"No, she has no devotion to one side or the other. She found them *before* the CIA and had her own plans for them. Problem is, she'll want them back. We already have those other killers on your trail. Ana Gray will only add to the misery."

Megan stopped eating. She sipped her coffee with alarmed eyes.

"You're gonna need a new face for sure," Raven said. "Maybe even two."

"Huh?"

"Or kill the doctor who does the surgery to make sure Ana or anybody else doesn't make him talk."

"Great."

"I'll pay her a visit and fix it."

"I'm not giving them back, Raven."

"Ana is the last person who should have them, don't worry. I want to find out if she'll tell me anything I can use to find out who took them to begin with."

He outlined his agenda to her. Raven didn't see a reason to hold back. If they knew what the other wanted, the exchange might help build trust. For now, he needed her to trust him.

RAVEN DIDN'T WANT to drive the Audi. He also didn't want Megan to think he was keeping her from leaving. Nothing would have stopped her had she wished to go again. She was resourceful enough to leave if she wanted, Audi or not. But like gifts at Christmas, the thought mattered most.

He took an Uber back to Sebastian's but could not bring himself to check the condition of the bar. There'd be crime scene tape and a police guard. Other shop owners might recognize Raven as Sebastian's tenant. He was taking a big enough chance collecting his car, which he'd rented under his own name. He found the car where he left it in the public parking lot and drove away.

He thought about Ana Gray. She wasn't easy to forget. She matched his six feet, and her ego overpowered even the slightest task. He'd never seen her without one of a large assortment of diamond necklaces. She had enough to wear a different one every day.

He reached the large house with its surrounding wall and balcony aimed at the airport. He pressed the button on the intercom at the gate. A man answered.

"Sam Raven to see the lady of the house."

"Ms. Gray is not here."

"Tell her who I am. She'll see me."

A few minutes ticked by. A buzzer sounded, and the gate swung open. Raven drove through. A guard met Raven at the front steps. He wore a pistol on his hip. He told Raven to face the car. Raven put his hands on the fender. The guard gave him a thorough pat down and didn't stop when he found the Nighthawk pistol. The search moved down the length of each leg and the man wasn't shy about pawing Raven's crotch.

"Is this necessary? Ana knows me."

"I have my orders," the guard said. He took Raven's gun. "Let's go."

Raven noticed more armed men milling about inside. Some carried submachine guns. The guard brought Raven to the third floor, a large room with wrap-around windows and the balcony. The guard departed; he didn't say how long Raven would have to wait. Raven examined the windows and thought about buying stock in Windex. With so much glass to clean, Ana Gray alone would keep the company in business.

The largest windows were the steel-framed sliding balcony doors. Raven stepped close to the glass. Barcelona spread out before him. A passenger jet thundered over the house heading for the airport.

"Most people would hate having jets fly over their home," a woman said.

Raven turned around. "Hello, Ana."

12

ANA GRAY WORE HER DARK HAIR TIED BACK, TIGHT-FITTING white blouse almost like a corset to accentuate what little she had up top. Black Capris rode low over the flare of her hips. To Raven, the Capris only showcased her skinny legs. Ana Gray walked on toothpicks. But she was worth billions, not unattractive otherwise, and always made the eligible bachelorette lists circulating through the world's wealthiest. And, of course, a diamond necklace encircled her slender neck.

"When you have the aviation bug," Raven said, "a spot like this is worth whatever it costs."

"I designed this house myself."

She approached with folded arms and suspicion. "What are you doing here?"

"Came to ask questions."

"About what? The only time I see you is when you want something, and it's never me."

"You had a break-in."

"Really? When did this happen?"

"Stop, Ana. Somebody cracked your box and took an envelope."

She laughed. "There's nothing wrong with my box." She patted her groin. "In fact, nobody's cracked it in a long time. Fancy a try?"

"You know what I mean."

"God, you bore me. Want a drink?" She pivoted and walked to the bar. Raven followed.

"It's gin and tonic or jump off the roof," she said. She sliced a lime, filled a glass with gin and tonic water, and Raven told her he'd have the same. She sliced lime again with such speed it seemed as she'd only flicked her wrist. She poured gin and added tonic without watching the bubbles. The fizz touched the brim of the glass but did not spill over.

"I am the world's best bartender," she said.

"Woefully undiscovered," Raven replied.

She handed Raven the glass. "Lots of practice. Comes with being rich and bored."

"Is the spy world no longer fun?" Raven took a sip and nodded his approval. Ego or not, she mixed a good drink. But Ana did not reply or depart the bar. She downed her entire glass, let out a breath as she set the glass down, and mixed another.

"If I'm not getting laid, I might as well get drunk." She sliced the lime again.

"Is that your answer?"

She filled her glass. "Bloody hell, it was never fun. But it was interesting. *Now* it's annoying."

They moved outside to the balcony. The umbrella extending from the center of a glass-topped table blocked the bright sun. A jet flew over the house and Ana paused to watch the plane. The sky was clear and blue, the breeze gentle. Raven sat and took another drink.

Ana sat and held her glass with both hands. "Tell me why you're here, Raven. Nobody knows what happened the other night except me and one of my employees, and whoever ripped me off."

"Word gets around."

"Bollocks. You're here to gloat. You were in on it."

"If you really thought so, you wouldn't have made me a drink. I'd still be at the gate. Or you'd let your guard keep molesting me."

"I poisoned your drink."

Raven laughed. "I watched you mix it, Ana. You'd roofie and rape me before ever poisoning my drink."

Ana's face turned sour. She looked at Barcelona instead of Raven. "Tell me what you know."

He said, "I know compromising photographs, never mind of whom, are, or were, in circulation. I know the CIA was looking for them. You got the pictures before they did. Then somebody told other interested parties. Two of said parties converged on your property at the same time. One successfully looted the booty."

"Damn you, Raven, you're teasing me. And I'm too mad to make a sex joke because you wouldn't laugh anyway." She faced him. "All of what you say happened, and now you show up."

"Here I am." He grinned.

"You have no idea how hard I worked to get those pictures."

"Only to be foiled by—"

"Somebody who I thought to be trustworthy. I'll tell you how it happened. My former employee, a butler, who was acting as security while I was gone, had it in his head he could make money at my expense. He let the thief into the house. Woman named *Megan*. Works alone, very crafty and all that. She left him out cold on the floor as well as *unpaid*, the little bitch."

"And your man?"

"Dealt with."

"If he told others you had the pictures, where did they come from to start with?"

"There are some in the American government who want to bring down the president. The pictures were how they planned to do so."

"You're joking."

"Nope. And the people who want the president gone weren't very careful. One of them, or more than one, talked. I swear you can't trust anybody these days. The FBI stepped in. Before the Feds arrested every member of the group, somebody sent the pictures into the wild. One way or another, they'd get what they wanted."

"And it became a free-for-all while the CIA busted heads to keep them out of the wrong hands."

"Yes."

"Wow."

Raven took a drink and thought over the scenario. It meant getting to the source was out of the question. But at least he knew who and why, despite the lack of names. Their names no longer mattered to him.

"It was glorious, Raven. I beat everybody to the prize. Then lost the damn things." Ana swallowed the remains of her gin and tonic and left the chair to return to the bar.

Raven looked at his drink. He'd barely finished half.

He had a new idea worth presenting to Megan. Offer to pay for her new face and identity in exchange for the pictures. Then she'd be out of danger, and he'd be on his own to deal with the men who sent the killers who murdered Sebastian. He owed Sebastian's father the effort, even if the son had been a pain in the neck.

Ana returned with a full glass and dropped into her chair again.

"I want the pictures back, Raven."

"No."

"Name your price."

"You know better than to make such a suggestion. What do you want them for, anyway?"

"Whatever," she said. "This and that."

"You're the last person who should have them."

"Aw, don't be mean."

Raven finished his drink and set down the glass. He stood.

"Leaving already?" Ana said.

"You say this thief, Megan, stole the pictures?"

"She or the other crew. They had a shootout on my lawn. The gardener had to get all the spent brass out of the grass before he could mow today."

"Be seeing you."

"Hey!" Ana Gray bounced from her chair. He turned. She pointed a finger at him. "If you won't get those pictures back, I have people who will."

"Tell your people if they tangle with me, I'll return them in pieces."

He turned his back and reached for the sliding door.

"Raven."

He faced her again. Ana held her glass in her left hand and swept up and down her body with her right. "How come you never want any of this? How many hints do I need to make?"

"Easy answer."

"What?"

"I'm not sure which one of us is the spider and which one is the fly."

She blinked with her mouth partly open.

"Be seeing you, Ana," he said. This time, he exited without interruption. He waited until he'd collected his gun and

turned the rental out of the gate before allowing himself a
laugh.

13

THE BOSS WASN'T GOING TO BE HAPPY.

Shaw dreaded the call he knew was coming. He was certain the man who hired him already knew about the failure and expected an explanation.

Logan Shaw let out a frustrated sigh and sipped his coffee. He sat in the back corner of a narrow sidewalk café. It was a hole in the wall, with gaudy paint slapped on the walls. The walls contained random decorations, scrap metal from a junk yard pieced together. None of it mattered to Shaw. He was alone, sitting with his back to the wall, and a half-wall in the middle of the shop concealed him from the front door.

Escaping the shootout at the bar had not been easy.

First, they'd had to leave Buchanan behind. He'd lost half his face in the return fire. The coroner would have to use his dental records to identify him. A lousy way for a decorated US soldier to end.

Second, with the rear tires of the van shot out, they'd had no choice but to abandon the vehicle too. All of their gear and gizmos were aboard. Shaw and Webb only retained their handguns and a small amount of ammunition.

The situation was bleak, yeah.

Shaw waited for Webb, who had ventured back to the bar to see if any of the neighboring shop owners had any news. Shaw figured the cops had the van. The car they had stolen from the public lot, an old '70s vintage Saab they had hot-wired, they'd ditched a few blocks away. Whether the police discovered useful prints on the vehicle was irrelevant. Once they put a name to Buchanan's corpse, Shaw and Webb would be implicated.

The trio wasn't exactly unknown. Their files occupied server space at Interpol.

Shaw drank some more coffee as he stared at the wall a few feet away. Ceiling fans stirred the warm air inside. Shaw still felt sweat on his neck. He had no idea how to proceed, and the boss would not appreciate the update. Not one bit.

Tony Webb stepped into the café and wandered through. He looked at faces until he found Shaw. He pulled out the second chair and sat. Webb sweated and breathed hard.

"Want a drink?" Shaw said. "Coffee is good here."

"This place ain't got nothing strong enough for me."

"Did you learn anything?"

"Bar's closed, crime scene tape, all the trimmings. The shop owners next door say the shooting was a break-in gone wrong. The bar owner Buchanan shot was Sebastian, and he was renting the top loft to the guy with the .45 auto."

"So, nothing."

"What helps the cops' theory about the break-in was this Sebastian fellow had a few grand hidden under the floor of his apartment, along with several illegal machine guns."

"What about the other man? The one who shot Augie?"

"No idea who the man was, his relationship to the woman, or anything to help soften the blow when Zupan calls."

"Or we call him. I think you're right. We need to go some-where else for a stronger drink than coffee."

Shaw left money behind and exited behind Webb.

They found a liquor store and brought a couple of bottles back to Shaw's hotel room. Neither wanted to be in public when Branko Zupan called. The Croatian mercenary phoned within five minutes, as if he had somebody watching. Shaw wouldn't put it past him to do so.

Shaw answered his ringing cell phone and switched the call to the speaker. He placed the phone on the table next to the bottle of Johnny Walker Red.

"Branko. Go ahead."

"You better have a reason for one of your men laying in the morgue right now."

"How did you know?" Shaw said. Webb took a long drink.

"I have people everywhere, Shaw. Now give me your report. I sent you on a simple snatch-and-grab and now we have multiple dead. Why?"

"Somebody else showed up at the British woman's house," Shaw began. He explained the events leading to Buchanan's death at the beach bar.

"Who was the woman?"

"I'd only be speculating."

"A guess is better than nothing right now, Shaw."

Shaw swallowed a mouthful of whiskey. Zupan spoke with a level voice, he wasn't yelling or frothing at the mouth. The muted approach almost made him sound angrier than if he *had* been screaming.

"I think it was Megan," Shaw said. "She's a thief who works alone, high-value targets, nothing penny-ante with her. Who the man was, we have no idea."

"Who is this Megan? Megan what?"

"No last name."

"She can't be too hard to find, right?"

"And if I'm wrong and we end up chasing ghosts?"

"Find her or you'll be joining Buchanan in the morgue."

The call ended.

Webb whistled.

"We're not wrong," Shaw said, "but she's long gone by now."

The two men sat drinking, and then Webb snapped his fingers.

"Our informant."

"You mean—"

"He told us, why not her too? You said the same thing when we ran into her."

"I'll drink to that." Shaw downed what remained in his glass. "Go back to your room and get packed. I want to be out of here in two hours, max."

Webb finished his drink, too.

MEGAN PACED THE KITCHEN.

She dared not go outside and kept the shades pulled down over the windows. She paced with the Beretta nine-millimeter on her right hip.

She'd cancelled her extraction team after Raven's departure. Told them to keep the money she'd paid them. She was out almost $5000 US, but the new life promised by her possession of the photographs made up for the loss.

The events at the bar, which took place in her absence, continued to bother her. She needed to help Raven track down the other crew. Help him avenge his friend. She felt responsible for what happened and wanted to do something to make up for her error. At least she had to try.

It was hard not to laugh at herself for the current line of thinking. Here she was engaging in do-gooder behavior she'd sworn never to do. Raven and his attitude, his loyalty, brought it out of her. The only other man to ever make her consider efforts not self-focused was Philip. She shivered thinking of how alike the two men were.

Her new identity would allow her to behave like a normal human more often but doing so in her current state made her vulnerable. The goal was to remain strong. Impregnable. A fortress of resolve. She had to stay safe.

A car pulled into the drive. Megan snatched out the Beretta and ran to the window. She parted one of the blinds. Raven stepped out of a compact Mazda sedan. She let out a breath and holstered the pistol. He'd told her he was going back for his rental, but the arrival still brought her combat senses to full alert.

She opened the front door. He didn't miss a step. His steady movement carried him through the doorway and into the house with a smile.

Megan closed the door and turned the locks. She was breathing hard.

"You all right?"

"I forgot you were getting your car."

He glanced around at the closed blinds, and all the lights, which she'd switched on to make up for the lack of sunlight. He looked back at her. She expected a remark about being paranoid and overreacting. He said, "Have you eaten?" instead.

"Lunch? No. Nothing since breakfast."

"Don't tell me you've sitting in a corner, gun in hand, the entire time I was gone?"

"Part of it."

He stepped forward with his arms open. She stiffened as he embraced her, then melted under his grasp. She returned the embrace before she could stop herself.

"It will be okay, Megan."

He was taller than her, her face buried against his neck. She felt the warmth of his body. "I'm sorry about Sebastian. I didn't mean—"

"I know." He broke the embrace.

She stepped back wishing it had lingered.

"Let's send out for something," he said, "and I'll tell you about Ana Gray."

"What do you want?"

"I don't know, what do you want?"

She frowned.

He laughed. "When in doubt, order pizza," he said. He went to the kitchen and filled a glass with water.

She followed, satisfied with the relief at his return, but still unsure if she should trust him. Fight or flight was in conflict with the first person to hug her since Philip died.

14

Raven gave her every detail of his conversation with Ana Gray. He talked while chewing pizza. By the third slice, he concluded the story.

"She gave me the background, but nothing to grab onto for a lead."

"Let me get this straight," Megan said. A piece of pepperoni dropped from her pizza slice and landed on her plate. She picked it up and ate it. "You're satisfied on the origin of the pictures and the purpose behind them."

"Correct. Dead end there."

"And now you're focus is the men who attacked the bar."

"Yes. Except—"

"What?"

"I should go after them alone."

"But, Raven—"

"You've done enough."

"What do you mean I've *done* enough?"

"Not—" He sighed. "My apologies. I don't mean it in a bad way. I mean you've stolen the pictures from somebody who would have sold to the highest bidder. You're done. The rest is for me."

"No! I'm not giving them to you and if you think—"

"Let me tell you my idea," he said.

"Um…okay."

"In exchange for the pictures, I'll pay for your new face and new name. You'll be clear of all this. I'll have the pictures and the trouble that goes with them. Then you get what you want, and I'll go get what I want."

Megan felt a rush of heat through her body.

"No, Raven. I'm staying with you. I owe you for…what happened."

"Megan—"

"No! Besides, without me you don't have anywhere to start looking for those guys, whoever they are."

"What do you suggest?"

"My informant. The one who told me about the envelope. He may have tipped the others too."

"Why?"

"Maybe they offered a better cut? It's worth a try."

"They might have tortured him for the info," Raven said, "and killed him."

"We won't know unless we check," she said.

He set down his slice and looked away from her. What was he thinking? She appreciated his offer. It was above and beyond, and if she wasn't as conflicted about her own feelings as she was, she'd have accepted. But her escape left a man dead who had nothing to do with the storm of violence she'd brought.

Or maybe she should take the offer, give Raven the informants name, and be done. One way to her goal was as good as another.

But there was honor and pride to consider. She wasn't callous and she wasn't a murderer. She had enough bad choices to live with. It might be nice to try and make up for one of them. She wanted to stay safe, but not at the cost of innocent people.

"All right," he finally said, facing her. "I understand. We'll see this through together."

"Good."

"Eat up. I'll handle our travel. I don't fly commercial."

Megan actually laughed. She'd expected as much. Raven didn't strike her as a man who took unnecessary chances either.

She gave Raven the rundown on where they needed to go. Her informant, an Irishman named Joey, had met her at a bar in Wexford, Ireland, to talk about the Gray job. Joey worked at the port of the coastal town. He kept a low profile while acting as a conduit of information to various clients.

Raven had never visited Wexford. Megan explained the town sat on the southern coast of the Irish mainland. Raven told her his visits to Ireland usually involved activity in the northern counties. He stopped short of providing more information. He said he didn't want to bore her with war stories

Megan decided Raven was different from Philip in one major way. He didn't talk about the past. Philip never hid anything from her. Raven clammed as soon as a hint of past experience came up.

She wanted to know more about him, though. Especially the locket he wore around his neck. What was inside, and why was it important to him? Perhaps on the plane he'd answer a few casual inquiries.

As promised, he'd chartered a private jet. The ride back to Barcelona, and the airport was uneventful. The shot-up Audi, still wearing its spare tire, remained at the cottage. Neither were in Megan's name. She didn't care what the police thought once the rental company reported the vehicle missing.

Raven returned his Mazda at the airport and a shuttle bus dropped them on the eastern side of the runway. A trio of private hangars sat with direct access to the departure lane. Dome-shaped, made of corrugated metal, they might have been supply warehouses. Raven steered her to the hangar in the center. It was their destination. The front sliding doors were open and the snout of a white jet, with a black stripe along the side, poked out.

"Are we flying a Lear jet?" she asked. He walked fast across the blacktop. Megan hustled to stay beside him.

"No, it's a Cessna Citation. Very similar. The crew works for me often and it's what they happen to fly. I like it. If they flew a Lear I'd like it, too. Doesn't matter as long as it has wings and goes places and doesn't crash on the way."

She had listened to Raven arrange the flight after lunch. He'd told the captain he was cutting his Barcelona visit short. He wanted immediate travel to Wexford for him, plus one. The captain promised take-off in three hours.

With his bug out bag over a shoulder, and Megan carrying her gear in a small tote, they stepped inside the hangar.

The Cessna Citation was narrow and sleek, the blunt end of the nose smaller up close. Four port and starboard windows, wider than what she saw on commercial airlines, stood out the most. The swept-back low-mounted wings also looked impressive, the design promoting streamlined aero-dynamics.

A blonde woman in a black flight attendant's uniform waited in the doorway. She had long hair and was too skinny. Megan thought her arms looked spindly. She greeted Raven cheerfully as "Mr. R." which amused Megan. She'd have figured on him preferring a less familiar greeting. Raven introduced Megan to "Miss Bridget". The flight attendant stepped back to allow them up a small set of steps and into the jet.

Megan frowned when she cleared the doorway.

Two rows of leather seats on either side of a very narrow cabin. Raven had to bend a little to a keep from bumping his head on the arched roof. Megan had no such difficulty. But she did have difficulty moving along the narrow walkway. She had to turn her body and move sideways, as did Raven.

Miss Bridget told them to get comfortable. They'd begin their taxi to the runway in ten minutes. She left the cabin for the cockpit.

Raven took a seat facing front; Megan sat opposite, her back to the flight deck. A polished wood-grain table rested against the fuselage wall. Raven showed her how it folded out between them, then put it back in place.

Megan cleared her throat. "Hope you aren't claustrophobic."

"It's a comfortable ride. Cramped, yes."

Raven turned his head out the window. In the distance, the main terminal building looked hazy.

"I'm going to miss this place," Raven said.

Megan grinned as a joke came to mind.

"The airport?"

"No, Barcelona. The city has charm." He looked at her. "Oh, wait, you're teasing me."

She laughed. "You said you were here to get away from something."

"And Barcelona seemed like the best place to do so, albeit I failed miserably."

"I'll never come back. I don't like returning to places where...you know."

"Don't dwell on what happened," Raven said. "You've

shared your perspective. It was an accident and might have happened anyway, and the reply is my responsibility."

"You really should be angrier with me." She felt herself sinking into the chair, as if she wanted to get away from him.

"Megan, I *was* you once. I understand more than you realize."

"Still—"

"And you wouldn't understand my reason either."

"Try me."

He shook his head.

She blinked at him. Raven remained silent. His attention was out the window again. But his gaze went much further than the terminal building in his line of sight.

Megan examined her fingernails for lack of anything to do. If she asked him a question about what he was thinking, he'd shut her down. Her gut told her so. She stayed quiet. The pilot spoke over the cabin intercom. "Prepare for departure." The engines flared to life. The interior insulation of the cabin muted the rumble.

The jet began to taxi from the hangar. Megan snapped her seatbelt across her lap. "Almost forgot," she said. Raven turned to her.

She said, "How much does it cost to travel like this?"

"Our flight to Ireland is $3000 an hour."

"Whoa."

"Worth the investment," he added.

"Where do you—" She stopped.

"What?"

"Get the money?"

He smiled and winked.

Megan let out a breath. He wasn't going to commit to a different answer.

15

RAVEN WATCHED HER. AS THE JET TOOK OFF, HER EYES widened. This might have been her first time on a private jet, but for him it was old hat.

He'd come to Barcelona to get away from himself. It was a silly concept to run from what you carried with you. He'd wanted to hide from the ghosts who propelled him through his war without end. They found him anyway. They had brought Megan to him. Sebastian had died to assure he didn't leave her. He fought for those without a champion who were victims of predators. Like the men who murdered Sebastian. If Raven had run, they'd continue their attacks on those without the means to fight back. His ghosts were cruel task masters, and it was the other reason Megan would not understand. Raven wasn't sure he understood himself. He had lived with his ghosts long enough to accept his reality. He had no choice but to respond to circumstances they carried him into.

Raven wasn't living the life he had wanted, but what he wanted he had lost. *Ripped* away, more like it, in a flash of sudden violence he'd been powerless to stop. Now there was nothing left to do but make the world's predator's pay. *Dearly*. With their own blood. He'd show them the meaning of the word *payback*.

He didn't know what awaited them in Wexford. But he planned to adapt and face the challenges head-on. It struck him their enemies might have the same idea. He and Megan needed to reach her informant, Joey, before the other side. He and Megan wanted to know who else knew about the contents of Ana Gray's safe. The other side wanted to know how Joey *reached* Megan. Raven only hoped they didn't have access to the same fast transportation as he did.

Then there was the added complication of Ana Gray's search party. She knew who she was looking for. She'd have her own resources to exploit. Raven hoped she remembered his warning, because he didn't want to add her to his enemies list. They weren't friends, but there was no reason for animosity between them. He figured she was smart enough to order her crew to hang back if they encountered him. What Ana Gray might say when she learned he already had Megan within reach he would deal with later.

For now, all he needed to think about was enjoying the flight to Ireland. And getting to know Megan better. Trouble followed at its own pace and would find him at the time of its choosing.

MISS BRIDGET, the skinny blonde flight attendant, served drinks. She mixed Raven a martini; gin, vermouth, stirred; while Megan was content with red wine. To her surprise, like Raven's martini glass, Miss Bridget handed her a real wine glass.

"You live a lavish lifestyle," Megan said.

"Hardly. The plane is a splurge. I have a house boat in Stockholm. It's not much larger than a camper."

"Do you like it?"

"The lake I'm on is nice. The marina has a social club. It has its perks."

"I don't take a lot of time to enjoy myself."

"Why not?" Raven asked. He sipped his drink.

"I move around a lot. Never stay in one place very long. I get anxious. I'm trying to stay one step ahead of the police in half a dozen countries and find ways to keep eating." She swallowed some wine. It warmed her stomach. "It's not much of a life," she added.

"With all your travel, you stop and smell the roses from time to time."

"More like a look over my shoulder as I pass by."

Raven nodded. "You ran from me but you came back. You broke the pattern. Why?"

"Well—"

"You told me it wasn't safe, and came back because I wasn't safe, either. Tell me more."

"I will if—"

"What do you want to know?"

"About your locket."

"Deal."

She took a deep breath. "I told you about somebody you remind me of. Another man who saved my life once."

Raven waited.

"It happened the night I got trapped in a church..."

BUT FOR THE story to make sense, she had to go back to the day the nuns made her leave the orphanage.

Two of the nuns escorted her down the steps to the sidewalk the day after her 18th birthday. She had the clothes she wore, a small suitcase with a few more, and the best wishes of old women who wouldn't remember her the second she vanished from their sight.

But Megan had planned ahead. She had no intention of living on the street. Instead, she secured a residence in a small apartment complex run by other orphans now on their own. They operated the building as a collective, banding together to form the family they never had. Or so Megan thought. Soon she'd learn the same abuse and mistreatment found in the orphanage waited for her at her new home, too.

Membership in the collective had a price. She'd need a job. They expected her to contribute a percentage of her pay to the others. Everybody worked to support each other so nobody went without. Or so they said.

It was fine with Megan. She didn't know any better and having a real bed was her only goal. She did not want to be on the street, sleeping in alleys or doorways. She did not want to be vulnerable to predators like too many others she saw.

The apartment complex wasn't huge. Many living there doubled- and tripled-up in the apartments to save money.

The paint on the outside walls, a faded tan, was peeling in several areas. The maintenance crew was too busy dealing with the grounds and infrastructure to tackle the paint. Inside, it was nicer, with a pool and spa. Communal dining if one wished to socialize, cooking facilities in each apartment if they didn't. Megan found most of the residents friendly but everyone seemed nervous, wary, uncertain. She dismissed this as the attitude of young people with no real experience in taking care of themselves. They were all learning with each new day; some of the older residents acted as counselors to pass on what *they* had learned.

It wasn't long before Megan heard of the dark side of the

collective. A man named Brandon served as the leader of the complex, and his icy eyes gave Megan chills. Upon meeting him, she learned the truth of the "contributions" each resident made. Brandon took the money. Everybody else paid for his stuff; he didn't have a job. In exchange he enforced the rules and made sure residents had protection. Megan knew all about "protection"—the protection lasted as long as you paid. Brandon kept up a nice facade, but it later cracked, and Megan witnessed it firsthand. He proved she'd entered not a sanctuary, but a nest of vipers amidst sheep.

Megan hit the street with her hustles and scams. She targeted the elderly and people who might have been the same age as the parents who abandoned her. She felt no guilt over taking their money and belongings. They owed her. They owed every abandoned child in Romania; Megan intended to make them pay.

She avoided Brandon but interacted well with the others. The ones going for the straight life, the normal life free of crime, ignored her. Except Philip.

She first set eyes on him in the complex recreation room, where he was shooting pool with other guys. He was two years older and limped from a childhood accident not properly addressed. He was also a strapping six-footer, cute and charming. She challenged him to a game, beat him, lost a rematch, but by then neither paid attention. They were inseparable.

Philip was trying to break out of his criminal habit. He'd been attending the local Catholic Church and listening to Father Ryan. The parish ran an outreach for the city's orphans with varying degrees of success. Philip's persuasion failed to get Megan to change her ways. Megan, like most of the others, was mad. Mad about being abandoned, abused, ignored. She had only started getting even.

Philip remained patient. Best of all, Brandon was afraid of

Philip. Every time it appeared a physical conflict might break out between them, Philip hit him with a "Let's go, Brandon," and a promise of a beat down. Brandon always backed off. His only explanation as to why they never went further was "we have an understanding."

All was right with the world, sort of, for a few weeks. And then one night Megan awoke to a scream.

She'd been sleeping alone, since Philip worked late, and first thought she heard the scream in a dream. Not an uncommon occurrence. As she awoke, the screaming continued. Her two female roommates heard the screaming too. They tried to keep Megan from investigating. She ignored them and dressed. They held her back from the door. *Let it go. It's nothing.* Megan knew it was something, and the reaction of her roommates only confirmed what she knew deep down. Brandon lived at the other end of the hall, and the screams were coming from behind his door.

She ended the protests of her roommates when she dug a pistol from beneath her pillow. Guns always shut people up.

Stepping into the hall, she heard the scream again. It cut off sharply. It wasn't a cry of sadness of anguish; the exact opposite. It was a cry of helplessness and terror.

The screams indeed came from Brandon's apartment. Three of his goons stood outside the door. She eased back the gun's hammer. The goons were standing guard, waiting their turn, or there to keep others away. Nobody else but Megan entered the hallway. The doors she passed remained closed. Perhaps like her roommates, they were too frightened to get involved.

The goons, as a group, turned to face her. They waited till she was closer before the tallest of the trio spoke.

"None of your business, Megan, go back."

"Or you might be next," said another.

They laughed.

They stopped laughing when Megan raised her gun and let the pistol speak for her.

She shot the tall one in the face and watched the bullet split his nose at the nostrils. The slug exploded out the back. Bits of Tall Goon splattered on his buddies, and as they jumped back yelling, Megan fired again and again.

Her second shot split the skull of the goon who said "you're next". The third bullet took down the last of the three, ripping a hole through either end of his throat. Goon Three collapsed against the wall making horrible choking sounds.

Three bullets gone; three remained in the short-barreled revolver. She tried the knob. Locked. She shot the lock and pushed through. Megan's eyes landed on exactly what she'd suspected, because she'd heard the same scream many times growing up.

An unconscious girl with her skirt and panties ripped away lay on a couch, a red welt on her face. Brandon rose from behind a chair and started to yell at her. The hot blood rushing through Megan made it impossible to hear. Her gun spoke once more. She shot him in the crotch; he cried out as he hit the carpet. She ran to him and shot him in the face. He stopped moving. Stopped his own screaming.

Time to run. She wasn't safe anymore. She had fooled herself into thinking she was when she wasn't. But she froze when she looked at the unconscious girl a second time. She was young, 13 or 14 based on her face and development. She might have been Megan once. Megan might have been her once. The shock was too much.

She ran back to her apartment but her roommates had locked the door. She bashed the doorknob with the butt of her revolver until it ripped from the door. Her roommates recoiled as she blasted through, hid as she filled a bag, and were out of sight when she ran out. But she hadn't forgotten to reload her gun.

Panic set in as she hit the street. Where to go? Somewhere Philip would know where to look. *The church!*

RAVEN INTERRUPTED HER. He said, "How long did you wait for Philip?"

"Too long," she said. "Brandon had more friends. They ran after me. Some on foot, others in a car. The ones in the car caught up with me first."

SHE WAS RUNNING, the street empty, clutching her bag close to her chest. Her right hand gripped the stainless revolver. The idea of running into a church with a gun in her hand didn't slow her down.

The racing of a car engine made her look back. Headlights brightened the dark street as the car sped toward her. She charged ahead. The church steps were only 25 yards away.

The car roared behind her. She jerked to the right as the vehicle passed, almost striking her. She felt the rush of air as the car went by. The driver slammed the brakes and stopped in front of her. As the doors opened, Megan fired one shot. She wasn't aiming, only firing into the car. A man screamed. She ran by, zigzagging. The engine roared again as the driver gave chase.

Megan bounded up the steps to the church and pushed through the thick wooden doors. She sprinted into the sanctuary, her legs aching, her lungs burning with strain. Megan shouted for Father Ryan. When she reached the altar, the priest appeared from a room off to the side.

"What in the world—"

"I need help! They're after me!"

"Who—"

The doors crashed open. Megan pivoted, dropping her bag, raising the gun.

"Get her!" somebody yelled as four men with guns of their own ran inside.

Megan's finger tightened on the trigger. The cylinder began to rotate.

"Megan, no!"

The revolver spoke in the darkened confines of the church. Flame flashed from the muzzle. One man down. She shifted her aim. Another fell as he dove for cover behind a pew; one ran outside. The last rose high enough to aim at her. Father Ryan jumped in front of her with his arms out wide, yelling for the violence to stop. She stepped around the priest and fired again. The last man let out a choked scream as her slug cored his face.

Father Ryan spun to her; his eyes were wide in fright. She let out a rush of hysterical words all mashed together as she tried to explain. This much she made clear. More were coming. She needed a place to hide. She needed Philip.

Before Father Ryan had a chance to reply, more commotion at the entrance made him turn back once more. Megan already saw the next wave of Brandon's goons coming for revenge. He told her to run. *Down the hall. Door to the back.* She bolted. She heard yelling behind her but the pulse beating in her head drowned out the words. At the end of the hallway, she spotted the door Father Ryan had indicated. As she neared, the door opened. She almost fell as she skidded to a stop and lifted her gun once again.

This time she didn't fire.

16

RAVEN SAID, "AND THEN WHAT HAPPENED?"

Megan had finished her wine. Raven waved for a refill. Miss Bridget came over with the bottle and poured more into Megan's glass. The flight attendant departed.

"Well?" Raven said.

Megan shook her head. "This is where it gets hard to talk."

Raven waited.

"The door opened," she said, "and it was Philip. I was right to run to the church. It was the first place he thought of too. He got home from work as the crew was running after me, and he hurried over. He grabbed me, we piled into his car, and drove off."

"Had to be tough. All this stuff—"

"Clothes, extra money, yeah, all back at the apartment. I had my bag with some money so we got a hotel. Then he started making calls. He was trying to leave his own criminal past with Father Ryan's help. But we needed to get out of the country. The police would be after me for murder."

"The church was self-defense."

"Brandon was not," she said. "His goons were not. I killed *four* men in cold blood, Raven."

"I know the feeling."

She sipped her wine. "Philip managed to get hold of some old contacts. We got passports through them. Then we left Romania."

Raven finished his martini and held the empty glass on his right leg.

"We moved around Europe," she said, "grifting and stealing. Short cons, long cons, the whole bit." She began to tear up. Megan wiped her eyes. "Somebody shot Philip later. Not during a job, but on his way to pick up dinner. Some drug addict in Berlin tried to rob him and shot him when he tried to fight. Dead on the sidewalk. Bang." She snapped her fingers. "Gone like when you blow out a match."

"I'm sorry, Megan."

"Yeah, well,"—she wiped her eyes and sniffed—"what would you know about it."

Raven used his free left hand to pull the locket from around his neck. He held it out to her. She hesitated, then took it. Using a thumb, she opened the locket one-handed. She gasped as she raised her eyes to meet Raven's.

"Is this—"

"Yes," he said.

"Oh, wow."

"They're both gone," he told her. "Don't tell me I don't know what it's like, Megan."

"I'm sorry." She handed back the locket. Raven clasped it tightly. She was the first person to see inside since he began wearing it. He never opened it; he knew who was in there.

"Well," she said, "now you know why I came back for you. I see Philip when I look at you. You make me feel...safe."

"Thanks, I do try." A smile tugged at one corner of his mouth. "Sometimes I fail."

"What happens when you do?"

"Try not to dwell on it or repeat the same mistake." A lie. But he didn't want to say anything to scare her. He needed Megan to remain level-headed till they had their current matter sorted.

"Where's the bathroom?" she said.

Raven pointed over his shoulder. He took her glass. She departed. He pulled up the table from its spot against the fuselage and set down the glasses.

He turned to the window. Scattered white clouds against clear blue sky and ocean below. He was glad she was opening up. And the world didn't end because he showed her the inside of the locket. He slipped it over his head to dangle below his shirt once again. He was used to it, and hardly felt the weight of the locket against his chest most days. But when he turned his head, he felt the chain dig into his neck.

They were both broken wings, he realized. Broken wings tended to attract one another. He couldn't get involved with her. This was a job. He wanted the pictures she took. He wanted a re-match with the men who killed Sebastian. And he didn't want anybody else hurt in the race to obtain the pictures. He'd see Megan to safe harbor, and then move on. Like always.

He lived by two rules. No roots; no gunfights in public.

Two rules. Two very simple rules.

But what if he broke rule one?

And who did he think he could break it with? Megan? He laughed. He spent too much time alone, he decided. That was his problem. So much time alone he had ideas about the first woman to cross his path.

Megan remained in the lavatory a long time.

Raven didn't blame her. He stayed in his seat, stared out the window, and tried to chase away the thoughts rolling through his mind.

THEY LANDED at Waterford Airport an hour away from Wexford. It was a small airport with construction on one of the runways. Megan explained they were widening the strip to accommodate larger airlines. The Citation had no trouble landing on the one available runway. The taxi to the small terminal only took a few minutes. Customs agents inspected their luggage. Raven once again blessed the X-ray proof compartments which fooled even the most careful search. Both sailed through to the front of the building.

No taxi cabs. Drivers collected other passengers, and the parking lot across the street wasn't full. Raven raised an eyebrow at Megan. She took out her cell and scheduled an Uber pick up. She told him the drive to Wexford offered plenty of scenery. The surrounding fields of green impressed Raven very much. If more of the same were on offer, the visit would be a nice one until work intruded.

The Uber followed the N25 to Wexford. Traffic wasn't heavy, and the open country dulled Raven's alertness. He welcomed the respite. The flat lands, open fields, farm land and occasional homestead reminded him life had a peaceful side. He needed to visit such areas more often. Batteries needed recharging. So did spirits. It wouldn't' hurt to leave the guns locked away now and then.

He glanced at Megan. She sat to his right in the rear seat. She took in the view with a relaxed gaze too. If he asked, she'd probably share his thoughts.

"Where are we going?" he asked. She'd given the driver an address but hadn't told him any details of the location.

"I keep a cottage here. On the coast."

"You like ocean views?"

She said yes. "The orphanage was in Constanta, if I didn't say so before. Near the Black Sea. The nuns used to take us there. I'd sit on the beach and wonder what was beyond the horizon. Had to be something better, right? I still wonder."

Raven only uttered, "Hmmm," in response. Something better indeed. Though he wasn't sure what. He hadn't discovered whatever "it" was and stared at the horizon a lot too. Maybe he never would find the answer, but he hoped to.

"I've always found the ocean calming, too," he said. "I think it's why I live on a lake."

They rode in silence some more. He wondered what life with Megan might be like. Would he welcome her new face? There wasn't anything wrong with the one she had, except others were looking for it. And planned to harm its owner when they found her. He had people looking for him now and then. Old enemies. People in need. A home base was a blessing and a curse, but a need he had no intention of denying. It offered some sense of a normal life.

They were two birds with broken wings in search of safety. Could they find it together? Raven wondered. Might he have a chance at future companionship, or was he made to walk alone?

He feared the answer.

17

ONCE THEY ENTERED CITY LIMITS, TRAFFIC REMAINED LIGHT, and Raven noticed more than anything the lack of skyscrapers interfering with the skyline. Megan explained the population barely exceeded 20,000 people. They had no need for skyscrapers. The tallest point in the skyline were the twin spires of a pair of Catholic churches.

They didn't turn downtown, but instead followed the R730 toward the edge of the River Stanley. As they turned off the motorway, Raven spotted the Wexford Bridge linking one side of the city to the other.

The driver turned left off the motorway. He followed a two-lane road lined with trees, and then the Pairc Charman football field appeared on the left. Megan said she could walk there to watch games. Raven understood more a moment later. The trees parted to reveal a small cottage overlooking the lake. Crosstown Beach sat on the other side of the lake.

The driver helped them with their luggage. Raven looked around as the compact car departed. The cottage wasn't unlike the AirBNB in Barcelona, but no carport. Instead, Megan had a side garden. But as Raven followed her to the front door, he had a closer look at the garden. Most of the life within was dying.

"Don't ask," she said. "If I was home more, I'd be a better gardener."

"You're kind of isolated here," Raven said.

"The football club used to be a school, and the head janitor lived in this cottage. They sold it off and I snagged it."

"Nice," Raven said.

They went inside and set their luggage by the door. Raven wandered while Megan set about opening windows and turning on the ceiling fan. The furniture was modest and unmatching; it looked as if Megan had raided a thrift store, and what of it? The couches and chairs appeared comfortable. The wooden coffee table had the required nicks and scuffs for added character.

He found her in the kitchen contemplating an empty refrigerator.

"We can have some stuff delivered," she said. "Won't take long."

"Is that safe?"

"Can't be paranoid all the time, Raven."

He pressed his lips together and nodded. It was nice to see a side of her not combat ready. But he figured she answered the door with a pistol behind her back.

She shut the refrigerator and frowned at him. "Something on your mind, Raven?"

He smiled and laughed. He didn't want to tell her what he was thinking. Two can cover the bases better than one. He said, "If you're taking requests, please make sure to include Irish Breakfast on the list."

"What kind of booze is that?"

Another laugh. She didn't smile. Her eyes narrowed a bit. She thought he was laughing at her, he realized. "It's a brand of tea, actually. While it does mix well with Bushmills or

Jameson, I don't make a habit of taking it that way in the morning."

"Ah ha," she said. "I'll make sure and get some for you."

"Where am I sleeping?"

"Down the hall. I'll show you."

He followed her.

Raven set out his clothes and gear while Megan used the phone to order the groceries. As he slid into the shoulder harness and put the .45 in the speed rig, he caught his reflection in the mirror. He shook his head. Megan might be a great girl but they were still too far apart.

He was there only to help solve her problem, deal with the men who killed Sebastian, and secure the pictures. Stick to the rules. Always. Rule One: No Roots. Don't have anything anybody can take from you. Rule Two: No gun battles in public. His job was to help and avenge victims, not create new ones.

Motion behind him. He turned to the doorway. Megan stood there. "Um…"

"What?"

"We need to talk about what to do with the pictures."

"Burn them."

"We can do so after I get what I need out of them."

"Do you have a safe deposit box?"

"I can get one," she said.

"They'll be okay one more night. First thing tomorrow, let's find a bank."

"All right."

"And then let's find your informant and get him to answer some questions."

WAS HE MAD AT HER?

Megan collected her bags and brought them to the master bedroom. She had to pass Raven's room again and did not look inside. He'd been a little too sharp in their last chat. He sounded upset. Or she was reading him wrong like she had about the tea. God, what an idiot she was. She should have known. Then again, she preferred coffee, so why should she bother to know various tea brands?

She set her bags on the queen bed and began unpacking. What she really craved was a shower and some time alone. Sam Raven was not Philip. Nothing she did or imagined would make him Philip. But as she started the shower and undressed, she realized she didn't want another Philip. God help her, she wanted Sam Raven.

No way. Whether he said so or not, he blamed her for Sebastian's death.

She stepped under the hot spray and closed her eyes.

MEGAN'S ONLY "BANK" was Bitcoin where she parked most of her money. The rest she kept in cash in a literal lock box buried in the garden. The box held various denominations.

Raven's only ID was his own and he wasn't going to put up such a red flag to their enemies who might look for such a sign. Megan had several IDs, so she selected one she hadn't used in recent weeks. They rented a car and secured a safe deposit box. She put the envelope of pictures everybody wanted inside.

Raven shut the door, turned the lock with the key, and held the key out for Megan.

"Keep this in a safe place."

She hesitated.

"What's wrong?"

"I guess I can keep it with my money."

"Sure."

She took the key. Their fingers touched. Her eyes flicked to his. Raven didn't feel a "spark" but her fingers were warm against his and he met her eyes. She broke eye contact to pocket the key and then lowered her eyes away from him.

She walked out of the vault room. Raven followed her.

18

THEY STOPPED NEXT AT AN ELECTRONICS SHOP. RAVEN purchased a pair of compact wireless cameras but didn't explain what he wanted them for right away.

There were two ports in Wexford. Rosslare Europort, a deep-water harbor for all major shipping. The other was Wexford Port, used for private and recreational boating activity.

Megan's informant, Joey, ran a bar near Rosslare Europort. All ports the world over see their share of contraband shipping. Wexford was no exception. Smugglers liked the town because it was small and off the radar. They thought it was safe, which also loosened their lips when they visited Joey's Place. Joey had the bar wired for recording to catch pieces of gossip.

They drove up and down the street in front of Joey's bar a couple of times before parking. Raven wanted to explore on foot. He and Megan hit the sidewalk and mixed with other pedestrians who them paid no mind. They browsed shop windows and goods on offer at sidewalk kiosks. Those were the obvious tourist traps. Raven noted more than one foreigner falling prey to the hustle.

Across the street from Joey's was another shop, this one a clothing store, and a dentist's office. An empty storefront he could rent to hide the surveillance cameras would have been ideal, but no dice. Raven found a second option almost as good. The alley between the clothing store and dentist's office would suffice. He examined the nooks and crannies of the alley. Usual debris. A fire escape climbed to the top floor of the dentist's building. Megan finally caught on with his scheme and said so.

"You want to hide the cameras here?"

"Yes. We'll watch for our friends and get good pictures. I can use those to get a positive ID."

"I thought the plan was—"

"Yes, we'll quiz Joey ourselves. But I expect they will want to know who else he talked to same as we do. Snapping their pictures will satisfy my need to find out who they are."

"You want to set them up now?"

Raven said no. They'd come back in the middle of the night when there was less chance of somebody seeing them. Raven wanted the cameras to have clear shots at the bar's entrance. With the conversation done, Raven suggested lunch. Megan thought lunch was a great idea.

Raven returned to the alley at three a.m. with Megan acting as look-out. The street was quiet and deserted. He noted a light on inside Joey's Place and figured the proprietor was staying late to finish the day's business. It did not slow him down. The cameras had charged batteries, and he knew where to install them. Zip ties held the first camera on the fire escape. He used an adhesive strip to secure the second to the cement ground near the mouth of the alley. Stray debris provided concealment. Discovery of the cameras did not concern him, and he would not return to collect the units. Each camera transmitted footage via wireless internet. He only needed to be close by to pick up the signal. For the purpose, he'd secured a hotel room down the block. He'd put a computer in the room to record the footage sent back by each camera.

All they had to do was wait.

Raven knew who to watch for. He'd seen the faces of the enemy in the lighted hallway of Sebastian's the night Sebastian died. When he visited the hotel room after breakfast the next morning, he ran through the footage. The enemy had rewarded him. Both men showed up, stayed inside about a half hour, and left. When they exited, remaining on foot, they talked. The visit was a recon and they'd be back. If they followed the same plan used in Barcelona, the pair would return at night, or in the early morning hours.

Raven took screen captures of the enemy's faces and forwarded them to a contact named Oscar Morey. He telephoned Oscar with instructions. His old friend and mentor promised to get back as soon as he had an answer.

He returned to Megan' cottage, showed her the pictures, and gave the update.

"What do we do next?" she asked.

"I'm not waiting for Oscar, or our friends. We need to grab Joey right away. Around closing time should be right. I expect our two friends won't be far behind us, so we'll need to work quick."

"Let's not kill him if we don't have to," she said.

"We won't. We don't need police sniffing around. He may still be of use, but he also needs a life lesson. As in, it's not good to antagonize opposing sides by feeding them the same information."

She smiled. "You're such a philosopher."

"No. I've been around long enough to learn whom not to

waste a bullet on. Pal Joey qualifies as somebody not worth the price of a slug."

————————

JOEY RIORDAN CLOSED his bar at two in the morning. He spent the next hour in his office reviewing the night's recordings. He played the sound files on the laptop centered on his messy desk. Other clutter filled the office space. He was blind to it.

Most of the sea smugglers and other nefarious types who visited the bar preferred the privacy of a booth. Every booth in the bar was set up with a concealed recording system. The microphones captured conversations digitally. Joey Riordan began with the first, the booth closest to the entrance, and listened to each sound file in turn.

Joey was a slight man with a lean build and dark hair. He was about as unassuming an Everyman as could be and had learned long ago the value of information. He'd worked on plenty of smuggling ships and knew how the crews liked to talk and blow off steam after a long voyage. His reputation as "one of them" made his bar an easy stop during breaks from sea.

The first few booths weren't exciting; mundane chats from regular customers. Presently he stumbled onto an awkward break-up conversation between a man and a woman. The fellow had a hard time explaining why he wanted to end the relationship. The woman, mad, berated him about being too scared to "come out and say it" and Joey laughed. He knew why the guy wanted out.

Joey finished listening to the recordings and deleted the lot. Nothing good tonight, which was the case 90-percent of the time anyway. It was always worth the effort to sift through when big nuggets turned up, like the info on what Ana Gray had in her safe.

Neither of the two who talked about the pictures had anything to do with getting the envelope into Ana Gray's hands. But they knew who did, and what Gray paid, and they lamented not being able to get their hands on some of the money.

He cringed. Thinking of the Gray situation reminded him of the visit from Shaw and Webb earlier in the day. The visit had not been pleasant or friendly. He hoped he didn't see them again.

He turned off the sound software on the laptop and opened a spreadsheet. Time to sort the night's take and see if he could pay the light bill for the month.

A knock at the back door sent a jolt of fear through him. His heart rate kicked up. Shaw and Webb had stuck a gun in his belly. No way was he going to let somebody into the bar not only after hours, but when he was alone without a weapon. The local cops did not look kindly on citizens packing heat. Shaw and Webb might have come back to silence him for good.

Another knock.

Then his cell phone rang.

19

JOEY YANKED THE PHONE FROM HIS FRONT SHIRT POCKET AS IF it were on fire. He looked at the screen. A number he recognized. It belonged to a thief named Megan. Why was she calling so soon after Shaw and Webb visited?

Only one way to find out.

"Hello?"

"Open the back door, Joey," the woman said. "Or I'll set your precious tavern on fire and the fire department can find your recording units."

Joey ended the call with a shaking finger and set the phone on the desk. He left his chair and office in a rush. He ran down a short hallway to the back door. He shot back the lock and turned the knob and then somebody kicked the door so hard the edge crashed into Joey's nose. He yelped and staggered back. He grabbed his nose with one hand, the pain forgotten as a man stepped into the hall.

"Poor baby has an owie," the man said. He reached under his jacket and took out a pistol. He held the gun on Joey's belly. Megan came up behind the man and shut the door.

"GET AGAINST THE WALL, JOEY," Raven said.

"You have the gun, mate, whatever you say."

Joey put his hands on the wall and leaned forward. Raven patted him carefully. No gun. He pressed the .45 into Joey's neck and told him to hold still. Megan slipped by. She spent two minutes rifling through desk drawers and checking the office. "Don't you ever clean?" Joey laughed. When Megan announced all clear, Raven shoved Joey through the doorway and told him to sit. Joey resumed his spot behind the desk but kept his hands flat on the desktop.

He eyed Raven with nervous tension. When he glanced at Megan, the Beretta in her hand made him gasp.

"We only want to talk," Raven said. "You had visitors. We'll call them Calvin and Hobbes. What do they have to say for themselves?"

"They're American mercs."

"Real names?"

"Logan Shaw and Tony Webb."

"What else?"

"I don't know anything else," Joey said.

"Did they talk to you or only scout the bar?"

"They talked to me. Shaw stuck a gun in my belly and Webb got a little rough."

"What did they want to know?"

Joey jerked his head to Megan. "How to reach her."

"And?"

"Let them know if she showed up with a new boyfriend. Figure you're the guy, right?"

Raven grinned. He looked at Megan. She was sweating, breathing hard. Her trigger finger tightened on the Beretta.

Raven turned back to Joey. "You told Megan about Ana Gray. Shaw and Webb, too?"

"They paid me a little more. But I didn't tell them she'd be there, too."

Megan said, "You didn't tell me either."

Joey gave her half a smile. The smile faded when he dropped his eyes to the gun in her hand.

"Do as you're told," Raven resumed. "Call them. We're going to have a nice get-together. Bring the Guinness."

"You make a strange request, mate. Do I call you after?"

"No."

Raven went around the desk. He lifted the .45 and brought the barrel down hard. Joey tried to block the blow, but the cold steel struck where aimed. His body went limp and he fell between the chair and desk.

"Come on," Raven said.

Megan followed him out.

SHE SAID, "I don't believe it."

Raven steered the rental car along the narrow streets of downtown. He drove slower than he would have liked. All the roads downtown and near the port were too narrow for any kind of speed. He didn't want to risk an accident by driving faster than circumstances warranted. His eyes darted between the road ahead and the rear-view mirror.

"What do you mean?"

"Everything I've done to stay hidden got wiped out because somebody stuck a pistol in Joey's gut."

"By the time we're done with Shaw and Webb it won't matter."

"But they can *tell* others. What if they spread the word as insurance?"

"Megan—"

"*This* is why I need to change my face. Get out of this life. Don't you *see*, Raven?"

"You couldn't keep your tracks covered forever. You should have changed your pattern on a regular basis."

"Sounds odd coming from you," she said.

"We have different goals. And I have friends to help. If they hear things, they give me a tip. It helps me to stay a few steps ahead."

"No way. I've always been on my own."

"Everybody needs somebody sometime," he said.

"What are you getting at, Raven?"

Raven opened his mouth to reply but stopped *Rule One: No Roots.* "Never mind," he said.

They passed through downtown Wexford and the road widened. Raven stepped harder on the accelerator.

Megan slouched in the passenger seat.

The last time she relied on help, she had Philip. But he was gone. She'd managed on her own for so long, she had to admit she had no idea how to open up to anybody. She'd been deliberate in remaining solo. After Philip, the idea of another companion, or even a friend, wasn't an idea she could grasp.

There was too much pain when things turned sour. Or the other person died.

She wondered if she'd have felt more control if she'd caught Philip's killer. The randomness of his fate made the search impossible. She'd have had to kill a hundred random drug addicts to hope she killed the right one. She built a wall around her instead, and now the wall had a crack.

Because of...

She looked at Raven. The road held his attention. He looked tense. Face stoic, lips pressed together. What was he thinking?

She faced forward again.

He slowed the car to take the exit leading to her cottage.

The refuge had been a safe place, but now a sense of dread took over. The cottage wasn't safe anymore.

She had to let him in.

Megan turned to Raven again but found no words to say. She let out a breath. Best to see how it played out instead.

20

A SHOWER MIGHT CALM HER, SHE DECIDED.

Raven announced he was going to make a cup of tea but she refused his offer of joining him. She left Raven in the kitchen. He'd removed his jacket but still wore his shoulder harness with the pistol under his left arm.

The spray did not settle her nerves and she shook under the blast of water.

She needed help.

No. She'd find a way to survive. She always had.

Megan turned off the water, dried with a big towel, and tied on a heavy bathrobe. She found Raven at the kitchen table with his steaming mug. He'd placed his gun in front of him. Megan went through the cottage checking the door and window locks.

"I've already checked," he said.

She ignored him and finished her inspection. He was right. All locks secure.

"I'm going to bed," she told him.

He lifted his mug in her direction. "Sleep well."

She went to her room and shut the door. More windows to check. All locked.

She needed control.

She needed help.

Dammit, she needed help *and* control.

Megan let the bathrobe fall to the floor and slid into bed. She stared at the ceiling for a long time.

Megan tossed and turned all night and awoke tired. She smelled bacon. Raven had breakfast and coffee ready when she walked sleepy-eyed into the kitchen. She poured coffee and sat at the table across from Raven.

"Trouble sleeping?"

"Mmmm-hmmmm."

Raven swallowed a piece of bacon and ate a bite of toast. "Everything's on the stove."

"Hmmm." She sipped her coffee and began to wake up a little more.

Megan felt more human after her first cup and put food on a plate and ate with Raven.

"You never told Joey how you'd reach him," she said.

"Does it matter?"

"I'm curious."

Raven shrugged. "Path of least resistance. We call the bar."

"Not from here."

"Not from here, indeed."

She ate quietly a moment. Raven used a slice of toast to scoop the last of his eggs onto his fork.

"If we know who's after us now, this Shaw and Webb, what good are the pictures you took?"

"Joey admitted not knowing anything else about them," Raven said. "My contact will find their entire history from birth, and we'll know who else they're working with."

"You don't think they're alone?"

Raven shook his head. "'American mercenaries', remember?"

"So?" She frowned.

"It's possible they're going for the retirement score same as you. It's also possible they were hired. I want to know for sure."

"And your contact can find out?"

"You'd be surprised what Oscar can find out."

"What about asking them? You know, tie 'em to a chair and work 'em over." She grinned.

"The next time I meet those two," Raven said, "there won't be any talking."

His words sent a chill along her spine.

"Where?" Raven said into the phone. He'd driven to a neighborhood of homes ten miles from the cottage. He sat curbside in front of house.

"They'll meet you tonight at ten o'clock," Riordan reported. "You're going to need to follow the R741 motorway to an open field off Orchard Lane. It's on the coast. George's Channel. There's a cluster of trees in the middle where you can meet and nobody will see you."

Raven weighed every word Joey Riordan spoke. He didn't sound nervous, but Raven decided it was no indication of duplicity. He was grasping for meaning where there might be none.

"Wait," Raven said.

He ended the call and search the location. He found the R741 and George's Channel and looked for the secluded spot Riordan referenced. It was a good spot. Far enough away to not endanger the public when the shooting started.

And Raven had no intention of leaving the meet with a clean gun.

He called Joey again.

"Tell them midnight or go to hell."

Joey said, "I'll tell 'em but they'll want to know why, mate. Is this only for a showdown?"

Raven had discussed with Megan an answer to the inevitable question. He didn't mean a word of what he said when he replied. "Tell them they can have the pictures in exchange for leaving Megan alone."

He needed Shaw and Webb to restrain themselves long enough for him and Megan to open fire. If they thought the meeting was a trade, their caution might provide the edge Raven wanted.

All he wanted was to get Megan away safe.

"Anything else?" Joey Riordan said.

"Change the time to midnight."

Joey laughed. Raven knew he knew it was a dumb request. Both parties would be early. A little posturing didn't hurt. And the other side expected as much.

"Hit me back in a half hour," Joey said.

Raven grunted and killed the connection.

They had to cross the Wexford Bridge and connect with the R741 motorway. Raven drove while Megan followed the GPS display on her phone.

"We'll be in the middle of nowhere," she said.

"No danger to anybody but us."

"All we have is our pistols. What if these guys have real hardware? Or backup?"

"Don't worry."

"Think they'll fall for our trick?"

"I hope so," he said. "As long as they hesitate a second longer than they should."

"Will we be early enough?"

"Two and a half hours should be fine."

"Is this where we joke about famous last words?"

"Better not," Raven said.

He drove on.

RAVEN CURSED after taking the Orchard Lane exit as directed. The headlamps of the rental shined on what he *didn't* want to see.

"Nothing but houses," he said. "Is the map out of date?"

Megan consulted her phone display. The screen's glow lit her face.

"No, keep going. It should open up. The marker Joey gave you is half-way to the coast."

If they continued driving straight, they'd roll off the edge into George's Channel in the Celtic Sea. Raven didn't dislike a dip on the ocean, but he had no plans for one tonight.

"Where's this magic marker?" Raven said.

"Straight ahead."

The headlamps landed on the cluster of trees as described by Joey Riordan. They sat off the road. The road forked at the trees, one stretch of pavement leading left and around, the other trailing past.

Raven took the left fork and followed the road around the cluster. He stopped. The roadway continued into the dark, stretching into the blackness at the edge of the coast. He backed up and returned to the main road. This stretch of pavement ended dead in a field of dirt. The lights showed flat but open ground. No trees. The only cover and concealment consisted of shrubs and rocks. And not very large rocks, either.

"This could turn into a real trap if we aren't careful," Raven told Megan.

She didn't reply and Raven didn't expect one.

"Where's an infrared scope when you need one," he said.

He'd like to know if there were snipers hiding in the field. Or in the trees.

Raven backed up the car, turned around, and eased into the cluster. He stopped the car on the soft ground and turned off the engine. He and Megan stepped out with drawn pistols and made a circuit of the area. No gunners hid within the mix of thick and thin trunks. The cool breeze from the coast did little to tame the heat Raven felt throughout his body. He felt sweat on his skin, his shirt sticking to his back. They were away from people, yes, but more and more it looked like an awful place for a confrontation.

"You okay?" Megan asked.

There's nothing else to do but play the hand. "Let's get comfortable," he said. "We'll be waiting a bit."

They split up after making a quick plan of action. Raven would hide in the field, Megan in the trees, and Raven would shoot first. The crack of the Nighthawk Custom .45 would be her signal to start shooting, too. With any luck, both Shaw and Webb wouldn't make three steps beyond their vehicle.

The glare from the city lights from the motorway messed with Raven's night vision as he lay prone in the dirt. But once the enemy showed up, the glare wouldn't matter. They'd be silhouetted in front of the lights. Easy targets. Then Raven checked his thinking. Nothing about this was easy. Shaw and Webb were dedicated fighters. They'd proven their desire to get the pictures from Megan one way or another. By any means necessary, preferably violent. They weren't going to show up unprepared. Raven had never felt outgunned when he only possessed his pistol, but this time, he wondered if it was enough.

And all because of Megan. Despite his best efforts, he was becoming emotionally attached to her. He knew he should fight the desire for her. He had his rules, and they'd served him well, never mind the loneliness such dedication brought.

He wanted to know if he could relax the toughest. *No roots.* He wondered if he could relax the rule with Megan.

None of his rambling nonsense mattered now. Once Megan was safe, maybe.

A pair of killers were on their way.

Raven had to concentrate on shooting before they did.

21

Megan wanted revenge. Her body felt flushed with heat. The anticipation of whacking Shaw and Webb—it was nice to finally have their names—was all she thought about. Where would their car stop? Did she have the correct angle? Yeah, Raven had told her to wait. How could she when the two knew her secret? And she still feared they passed along what Joey told them. They'd have compatriots to pick up where they left off--maybe. It was the maybes and what ifs which bothered her most.

She lay on uneven ground. She'd selected a big tree for her hiding spot. The thick roots beneath caused the ground at the base to rise; then it sloped. The discomfort didn't matter and she dared not move now since she had blended with the environment. The shadows. The insects populating the area had grown used to her presence. Their normal activity might lull Shaw and Webb to a false sense of security. The notion they had beaten their quarry to the meet.

It was hard not to let her mind wander as she waited. For somebody who claimed to trust no one, and not want any help, she'd sowed the seeds of her own destruction. She'd trusted Joey with how to find her.

It was the damn pictures. She wanted them as bad as everybody else, and the chance for a fresh start had clouded her judgment. And who could have expected such a disaster anyway?

None of this would be happening if she still had Philip.

But he was gone. No amount of wishing was going to bring him back.

She might find the same reassurance with Raven, though.

He had built the same wall around himself as she did. He might not admit to doing so, but there was no denying the truth. They were a lot alike. Birds with broken wings looking for a place to land.

What if they tried to find sanctuary together?

Except now wasn't the time to ask. In the back of her mind, she still wondered if he was only helping her to steal the pictures for his own use.

He'd had the opportunity several times already. Unless he found an alternate way into the safe deposit box, they were still hers.

She'd know the truth about his intentions soon enough.

The wind picked up. Leaves rustled above. A new sound carried with the wind. The sound of a car motor.

And the motor grew in volume the more she listened.

Megan pushed off the safety on the Beretta and rested her finger on the trigger. She heard Philip in her head telling her to keep her finger away from the trigger until she was ready to fire. She *was* ready. More than ever before. The rage within wasn't as hot as when she'd discovered Brandon raping the girl in his apartment, but close. This time, she felt more control. When she fired, she'd be doing so with thought instead of anger. She'd shoot with the full acceptance of her actions leading to the deaths of others.

TONY WEBB STEERED the car along Orchard as he and Webb neared the cluster of trees.

"Kill the lights!"

The sharp command from Logan Shaw in the passenger seat jolted Webb into motion. Without a second thought, he grabbed for the left column stalk. He flipped the headlamp switch toward him. The front lights winked out.

Webb pressed on the brake pedal, shifted to reverse, and backed up. He drove backwards for ten yards and stopped.

"Far enough?" Webb asked.

Shaw yanked his Glock-17 from under his coat. "Split up. Try and take the woman alive."

"Got it," Webb said.

The mercenaries exited in a hurry, dropping onto the dirt. They moved away at a crawl, knees and elbows digging into the ground. They left a trail like the wake of a boat. But they were already under unseen guns. The trail didn't matter.

The first two shots came at Webb, who rolled left, grunting as the rough ground battered his body. The rounds smacked into the car. Glass shattered. Webb aimed his own pistol at the trees but the low light worked against him. He had no idea where to find the shooter.

"Tony!"

"I'm all right!"

"Where's the shooter?"

"Trees!"

Another blast. Heavier caliber than the first. Webb searched the trees for a muzzle flash. None. He realized the shots came from the opposite side of the car. Shaw's side.

"Move!" Shaw shouted.

Webb rolled left, winding as sharp rocks poked through his clothes. He fired three times at the trees, altering his aim for each shot. He wanted the shooter to hide for a moment. Long enough for him to rush forward. Webb estimated 25 yards between him and the trees.

Webb bolted to his feet, ran hard, and counted three seconds. At three, he dropped and rolled to the right.

Perfect timing. Two more rounds flashed over him. This time, Webb spotted a muzzle flash. He extended his Glock and fired back.

A woman screamed.

RAVEN CLENCHED his jaw as Megan fired. *Dammit!* He held back his own fire as the two mercenaries blended with the ground shadows. He wasn't going to shoot only to miss. He had to make the rounds count. He had to be closer. Look his target in the face. Look straight into his eyes.

He'd deal with Megan jumping the gun, literally, later.

The merc who exited the passenger side left his door open. The pair had disabled the overhead light on the inside. The lights in the distance also didn't help the way he thought they would. The shadows cast by rocks and the rise and fall of the ground did not look like the shadows cast by a body. The mercenary knew how to use the environment to his advantage.

The two men yelled to one another. A shape shifted. Raven looked using his sensitive peripheral vision. He didn't dare look straight ahead and risk missing a clue. His outer vision would pick up any disturbance, and when it did, Raven prepared to fire.

He held the Nighthawk .45 in both hands. The glowing night sights lined up as needed. He fired once. A test shot to see if he had been right. The round punched through the car, but his target yelled again to his partner. Now Raven caught the movement of a man crawling. As he topped a rise, and silhouetted against the body of the car, Raven tightened his finger on the trigger.

Another pair of shots from Megan. Raven didn't fire. His target rolled, blending with the shadows once again. Raven cursed. She'd ruined his plan. And Raven knew there was only one way to finish. He had to get closer.

He left his spot, zigzagged two seconds, and dropped. A bullet split the air above him. He rolled right as two more shots snapped his way. He fired back, ran forward again, and dropped. A roll to the left this time. His target rose, ran; Raven fired. The .45 slug kicked up a spray of dirt between the man's ankles. The man continued his rush. Raven jumped up and ran to meet the charge. The two men collided with grunts of aggression. Raven kicked and swung his pistol. His opponent blocked and struck back and Raven swept the man's legs from underneath him. They both landed on the dirt.

Raven saw enough of the man's face. Shaw! The boss of the trio. Shaw struck with his left fist, Raven ignoring the blow as he countered with a left elbow strike. Shaw tried to wedge a knee between them but Raven shifted his weight to block the move. Shaw freed his right hand, the one holding his Glock, from where it had been pinned beneath him. He swung for Raven's face. Raven blocked Shaw's arm. The gun fire near Raven's ear, the sound deafening, Raven's reaction one which gave Shaw another chance. As Raven winced from the detonation, his grip on Shaw slackened. Shaw again tried to get a knee between them. He succeeded this time and shoved his kneecap into Raven's gut.

Raven stifled a cry and slammed his head into Shaw's nose. *Snap!* Blood poured through Shaw's nostrils into his mouth. Shaw let out a choking sound as he sucked blood into his mouth. Raven made a knife-edge with his left hand and chopped Shaw in the throat. Shaw's eyes widened as he uttered another strangled croak. Raven rolled off, staying on his side as he extended the .45 and shot Logan Shaw in the head.

Raven's left ear burned. He felt around the lobe. No blood. But the ringing in his ear left him unable to fully hear. He rose and slapped a fresh magazine into the .45 and ran for the trees. There was still Tony Webb to deal with, and Megan was on her own.

Why hadn't she stuck to the plan?

22

MEGAN BEGAN BREATHING FAST WHEN HER SHOTS DIDN'T connect.

Then her target fired back.

The bullet came close. It *thwacked* into the tree she hid behind, pelting her face with shards of bark. She screamed. Not in pain, but in surprise. She looked forward again. Her opponent was up and running.

She fired three times fast with one hand, her arm shaking, every shot missing. Webb entered the cluster. She left her tree and shifted right, probing with the hot muzzle of her pistol. Webb dodged from tree to tree. Megan fired when she saw him, always too late, and then he ran in a flash toward her and batted the gun out of her hand.

Megan screamed as he hit her next. He grabbed a handful of her hair and pulled hard. She fell, Webb landing beside her on his knees. He jammed one knee into her stomach and hit her in the chest with his gun. Air left her. She opened her mouth wide but struggled to breathe.

"I want the pictures!"

She felt her cheek singe as he pressed the hot gun muzzle to her skin.

"Where are the pictures!"

"Here," Raven said.

Megan watched over Webb's shoulder as Raven appeared. He leveled his pistol. Webb tried to pivot; he made a half-turn, bringing up his gun, but never fired. Raven triggered the Nighthawk. The back of Webb's head split from his skull. Megan felt blood and pieces splash on her. Webb fell over and remained still.

Megan struggled to her hands and knees and tried to breathe. Raven helped her up. She leaned against him on the way back to the car. By the time she dropped into the passenger seat, she could inhale again. But her stomach and chest hurt. The pain throbbed.

Raven started the car. She might be breathing better, but Raven was still trying to catch his. Sweat coated his face. His clothes were dirty and his face showed the red marks of a hand-to-hand fight. He remained stoic as he backed out of the trees.

Pulling onto the road, he turned the car back the way they'd come.

"Raven—"

"Not now."

Raven drove. Megan waited fifteen minutes before trying to talk again. She didn't want too much time to pass.

Raven drove fast, weaving around other cars, keeping the rental's speed above the limit.

"Do I get to explain?"

"You fired first because you were angry, I get it."

"There's more to it--"

"Later, Megan."

"Why?"

"Somebody is following us."

Megan moved in a flash, twisting in her seat to pull the Beretta 92 from her side. She popped out the magazine to check the load and slapped it back into place.

"Take it easy," Raven said.

"They had back-up?"

"Makes no sense. They didn't show during the fight. But this pair of headlights have been sticking with us." Raven's eyes darted between the road and the mirror.

"What are you going to do?"

"Lose them. Hang on."

Raven slowed and moved across the road to the right lane.

He hooked a right after the next exit. Through an intersection and into a mostly-empty parking lot of a shopping center. He steered around the back of the building, stepping on the gas to reach the other side as fast as he could. Turning left, he cruised along with traffic. Megan turned in her seat to look back but had no idea what type of car she should be watching for. Raven hadn't said. In the dark, all the bright headlamps behind them looked the same.

"Are we clear?" she asked.

"Put the gun away," he told her. "I think we're fine for now. But there's another problem."

Megan didn't bother to holster the Model 92. She hammed it under his left thigh instead.

"What now?"

"I have no idea where we are," Raven said. "Please activate the GPS."

He grinned at her. She didn't think there was anything to laugh about.

THE LONGER RAVEN took to cool down from the fight the less he was mad at Megan for wrecking the plan. He knew most plans failed after the first moment of contact anyway. Once the plan went out the window, you had to improvise. Despite feeling banged up and almost getting his ear shot off, Raven felt they'd done okay. The mercenaries were dead. He and Megan still had the pictures.

But who was following them?

Megan used her phone to direct Raven to an alternate motorway and back to the cottage. Raven helped her check the locks and windows. She suggested they sleep in shifts. Raven volunteered for first watch and Megan went to bed.

Raven made tea and sat at the kitchen table. If Shaw and Webb indeed had back-up, it made no sense why the extra gunners hadn't joined the fight. Another answer occurred to him as his tea cooled. Raven dialed a number on his cell. The other end, in Barcelona, rang.

And Ana Gray answered.

"Hello, Sam."

"Did I wake you?"

"No, but you did disturb me. I have a new hunky dude here and he does all the things you're afraid to do."

"If he were so exciting, you'd have let the phone ring."

"For anybody but you, darling. Better hurry and tell me what's going on."

"Do you have anybody following me?"

"I have no idea where you are, darling. The answer is no. Do you think I'd forget what you told me?"

"Forget, no," Raven said. "Ignore, yes."

Ana Gray laughed. "I listened to every word, darling. I have nobody watching you for any reason whatsoever."

"All right."

"You don't sound all right. Do you need a few extra guys?"

"No."

124 | BRIAN DRAKE

"Because you don't trust me, right?"

"Yes."

She laughed again. "They'd be under your orders, not mine. The offer is good whenever you change your mind."

"Go back to your shower head, Ana."

"You ass!"

Raven hung up.

He tried a sip of tea. Still too hot. He put the mug down again.

Did Shaw and Webb have a back-up team or had somebody else picked up the trail? He needed to find the answers fast. The odds were going to turn against them at some point. When it happened, Raven knew he couldn't guarantee Megan's safety.

23

MEGAN ROSE AFTER A FEW HOURS AND RAVEN SLEPT TILL NINE. He went down the hallway to find out why she'd let him sleep so long, he found her snoring on the couch with her gun in her lap.

He shook his head and stifled a laugh. Well, they'd tried. And nobody had fired missiles through the front door so maybe they had been overcautious.

Raven drank a glass of water and then went outside. He walked around the cottage checking for any signs of disturbance. He found nothing but the tranquility Megan had wanted when she settled in the cottage.

The sports field across the way was where all the noise was, and while his left ear still hurt, it didn't ring anymore. The field was full of players in red, orange, and yellow uniforms. They'd broken into small groups to practice kicks and tricks with footballs.

Raven's phone rang. He grabbed it from a back pocket and answered. "Oscar," he said, turning back to the cottage, "guess what?"

"What?" said Oscar Morey, who never played along with Raven's guessing games.

"Those two guys I asked you about are dead."

"Why waste my time then?"

"It isn't wasted. I have other questions."

Oscar Morey, Raven's friend, sort-of intelligence chief, and personal mentor, hadn't always worked on the side of the angels. He liked to joke, when dealing with Raven, one never knew what side he was on either.

If questioned about his association with Raven, Oscar Morey would deny knowledge of his whereabouts. Raven expected and encouraged nothing less. For Oscar's own safety, it was important. Raven often targeted the type of criminal Oscar had once been.

Morey had traded his position as a high-ranking member of the European underworld for a more lucrative job. He was now an information broker with a reputation for keeping his mouth shut. With eyes and ears in a variety of dark places, Oscar Morey had no trouble compiling a terrific amount of information in a short stretch of time.

He and Raven were friends now, but Raven didn't like to reflect on how they first met. They might have killed each other.

Years earlier, Raven arrived in Paris to kill a man responsible for several murders. Morey intercepted him with a warning. The killer was part of Morey's organization, and the crime boss didn't want Raven nosing around. "Stay out of our business. You don't want this kind of trouble." Raven explained why his target had to die and drew Morey to his side. The killer had crossed a line, and some crimes were too heinous for even Morey to tolerate. He allowed Raven to finish his mission.

Their second meeting went a little better. Raven saved one of Morey's kids from certain death, and the underworld legend pledged his support. From there, the bond between them grew stronger. Raven was smart enough to know when fortune handed him a talisman. In this case, a crusty old bastard named Oscar Morey.

"What else do you need?" Morey said. "Shaw and Webb and their other partner, Buchanan, have a long history."

Raven sat on the porch step. "Tell me what you know."

"They're Americans."

"Right."

"All three met in the Marine Corps and went AWOL during the mess in Afghanistan. Still wanted for desertion, by the way. They started working as mercs after the withdrawal."

"Any regular employers? I'm trying to figure out if this job was of their own design, or if somebody gave them orders."

"Oh, they found a benefactor," Morey said. "With warrants for their arrest, they plugged in with protection quick."

"I need a name, Oscar."

"You're pushy today."

"My apologies. It's important."

"What's her name?"

Raven paused before replying. He wasn't surprised Oscar had figured out the situation without him having to say a word.

"Her name is Megan. Our late friends specifically targeted her, never mind why. I'm trying to pull her out of the fire."

"All right, stay cool. Their boss is another mercenary. A Croatian named Branko Zupan."

"Tell me about him."

"He runs a small outfit for a Dutch syndicate. I'm still tracing the Dutch angle, though."

"Where is Zupan right now?"

"No clue," Morey said. "Every source I spoke with says he's always on the move."

Raven closed his eyes and sighed.

"You okay, Sam?"

"Anything else?" Raven said.

"Sure. Zupan works with his girlfriend and her sister. All three made it through the Balkan war and now they're fighting for money."

"Oscar, I have another favor to ask."

"Whatever you need."

"I need to bring Megan and a package to you for safe-keeping. The package is the reason Megan is a target. Zupan and his crew may already be onto us."

"I'll be here. Ring the bell when you arrive."

"Okay."

Raven stopped talking. The silence only lasted a moment.

"Sam?"

"What if I broke one of my rules, Oscar?"

"Depends on which one."

"You know which one."

"Is she worth it?"

"She might be," Raven said. "I don't know. I'd like to find out."

"We've had this conversation before."

"Yes, we have."

"And I've told you—"

"No man should be alone."

"The real question is, can she keep up?"

"Yes. She already has."

"Then it won't hurt to try."

"But, Oscar—"

"Sam. You gotta bury the past sometime. Maybe now's the time."

Raven nodded to himself, letting Oscar's words bounce

through his head. His desires meant nothing if Megan didn't reciprocate; he might be fretting for nothing.

"I'll talk to her on the way to you," he told Oscar.

"Can't wait to meet her."

"See you soon."

Morey said good-bye and Raven ended the call.

He opened the door to go inside but stopped short. Megan backed away from the window left of the door. She stared at him with wide eyes.

"Raven—"

"How much did you hear?"

She swallowed. "Everything."

"Megan—"

"Why haven't you left?"

"What?"

"Shaw and Webb are dead. You avenged your friend. Why are you still here?"

"I told you I want to help you."

"And now you want to take me to your pal on the phone?"

"Oscar can protect you while I go after Shaw and Webb's boss. This isn't over."

"Well, it is for me," she said. "Go do your hunting by yourself. I have the key to the safe deposit box. I'll handle it from here."

"Megan--" He stepped toward her. She moved back.

"No! I can't do this, Raven!"

He reached her and she didn't pull away. He placed his hands on her shoulders. Megan turned away.

"Megan. Look at me."

She met his eyes. Hers were wet.

"Let's not be alone anymore."

He pulled her to him and kissed her. Her stiff body relaxed. Megan threw her arms around him and kissed back with more force than he anticipated, mashing her lips to his.

Raven broke the kiss to bend down and scoop her off the floor. She held on tight, her eyes not leaving his face, as he carried her to his bed.

They hurried out of their clothes. Megan stretched out on the bed, legs open and arms up, gesturing for Raven to join her. He supported himself over her on knees and elbows. He planted kisses on each side of her neck, moving down between her breasts as she gasped and shifted. Her nails dug into his skin. He slipped inside her with a slow thrust. She arched her back, opened her mouth to gasp, then urged him on with quiet whispers. She wrapped her long legs around his back. Raven felt a hot flush crawl up his neck; the same happened to Megan. She met his movements with thrusts of her own, and he drove deeper until they both exploded with delight. They rolled over and clutched each other. She buried her face in his neck.

"Don't let me go," she said.

"I won't."

24

THEIR INTERLUDE DID NOT LAST MORE THAN THIRTY MINUTES. Megan nudged Raven and suggested they get going. She showered first while he called his flight crew. They promised to have the plane ready when he and Megan arrived.

He waited in the living room for Megan to finish.

Having never crossed paths with the mercenary named Branko Zupan, Raven had little to work with. The man had covered his existence well. Raven hadn't heard of him before his chat with Oscar, either. He didn't know how Zupan operated, who backed him, or any details to help create a strategy.

The only choice was to follow the basic protocol. Get Megan under Oscar's protective wing before Raven and Zupan clashed.

Megan left the bathroom to dress in her bedroom. When she came out, she said she'd fix something to eat while Raven showered.

He didn't take long, put on fresh clothes, and packed his gear. He and Megan ate sandwiches while standing in the kitchen, and then he helped her pack. They didn't talk, but their eye contact spoke volumes. It was different between them now, and neither wanted to fight anymore.

Megan said she was sorry to be leaving the cottage for good, but she knew better times waited ahead.

Lastly, she dug up the lockbox of cash in the garden, put the safe deposit key in a pocket, and joined Raven in the rental car. She didn't look back as he drove away.

MEGAN WATCHED the scenery go by.

Her stolen moments with Raven lifted the weight from her shoulders. She wasn't alone anymore. The burdens of the past were no longer on top of her mind.

She felt free of the mind trap she'd been living in for far too long. Who knew how long it would last?

Raven said, "We do this in a flash," as they approached the bank. "Bank, airport, out of here."

"Where is Oscar?"

"Somewhere in Europe is all I'll commit to," Raven said. "He has a heavily-armed crew to keep the bad guys away. They'd have to be suicidal to try anything."

"I'll take your word for it."

Raven parked on the street a few doors down from the bank.

"Oscar is a good man. We've known each other quite some time."

"How did you meet?"

Raven laughed. "I'll tell you the story another time."

"I'll look forward to it when you come get me."

She reached for his right hand. He let her take it. When she squeezed, he squeezed back.

The bank stop took fifteen minutes. Every teller had a

customer. They retrieved the envelope of incriminating pictures and hit the road again.

Raven drove while Megan sat shotgun with her Beretta 92 tucked under her right thigh. The envelope sat in her gear bag stowed in the trunk.

Raven moved along with traffic with an eye on the motorway ramp a couple of blocks ahead.

An SUV weaved through lanes, the driver moving with aggression. Raven felt his combat senses switch to red alert.

He steered into the left lane and sped up.

"What is it?" Megan looked back. "The SUV?"

"Two men in front."

"I see them. One looks like--shit, Raven, he's sticking a gun out the window."

Raven turned the wheel as he clamped a hand on the horn. His speed forced the other drivers to move. He had to stay in the right lane now to make the on-ramp. He didn't want a fight on city streets and wasn't sure a fight on the motorway was any better. But for sure there were too many bystanders in the crossfire if they remained where they were.

"Raven!"

"I see them!"

The SUV swung into the second lane from the right, easing up on Raven's left rear quarter.

Megan unlatched her seatbelt.

"Stay there," Raven told her.

"They'll wipe us out!" Megan slid between the front seat to the back with her gun in hand. On her knees, left hand on the backrest, she flicked off the Beretta's safety switch.

"Stay down!" Raven shouted.

The passenger in the SUV stuck out a full-auto FN-FAL carbine with a folding stock. He fired a burst. The rental's back glass popped, slugs grinding through the metal body.

Megan bashed a bigger hole in the back window and fired twice in return.

Raven sped through the last intersection before the on-ramp and caught the ramp with ease. The SUV stuck close behind. Megan fired again but missed. Raven shouted for her to hang on while he made the tight right turn on the clover-leaf. He pressed the gas pedal to merged onto the motorway.

Megan fired through the back glass. Automatic return fire from the SUV's passenger drowned out the straining rental's engine.

Raven cursed. He was going fast, but the SUV kept pace. He weaved, Megan shouting for him to hold still. He did and she let the Beretta 92 do her talking.

The SUV backed off and swerved left and right, almost colliding with another car. Drivers scrambled out of the way. Megan's salvo cracked the SUV's windshield; her shots at the front tires sparked off the asphalt.

The Beretta's slide locked back over the empty mag. Megan grabbed a spare from her jacket and reloaded.

"My side!" Raven shouted.

The SUV pulled alongside the rental. Raven pressed the gas and surged ahead, but the SUV matched him once again. Megan didn't lower the back driver's side window. She fired through the glass. Four shots punched a hole in the window, two more smacking the passenger door of the SUV. She leaned forward to raise the muzzle and get a better shot at the passenger. The passenger twisted his body to aim his FAL at the rental.

The gunner in the SUV fired another full-auto burst. Bullets shattered what remained of the window in front of Megan. More high-velocity rounds punched through her chest. Solid smacks into soft flesh. She screamed and fell across the back seat.

The SUV crashed into the rental, Raven struggling to stay

on the road. He shouted Megan's name but she didn't respond. Another heavy jolt sent the rental off the road. The car drifted across the right shoulder, bounced, and tumbled over. It rolled once, twice, the roof caving in, a shower of broken glass flying around Raven. The seatbelt held him in place and he tried to keep his hands in front of his face. The front and side airbags cushioned the blows but he still felt every impact up and down his body. It rolled a third time and then landed on its wheels.

Megan's body left the seat, hit the roof, bounced off the seat again, as the car rolled. Her body came to rest at an odd angle on the back seat. A large amount of blood spilled from her torn body and covered the back of the car.

Raven's vision spun and his face hurt from the airbag explosions. Panic set in. He had to get out. The seatbelt came free easily despite his shaking hands, but the door wouldn't open.

The SUV pulled over ten yards ahead.

Raven groaned. He slid across the center console to the passenger door, which opened, and rolled out onto the grass.

Another car pulled up behind the rental. Raven focused fuzzy eyes on the three occupants. Two women and a man. They remained in the seats and watched. Raven turned to the SUV. The men exited, one cradling the FAL carbine and the other toting a stubby MAC-10.

Raven rose to his knees and pulled out the Nighthawk .45. He fired once. The driver's head snapped back and he dropped.

Raven rolled deeper into the grass as the passenger raised his FAL. Raven fired again and again. Each .45 hollow-point tore into the gunner's chest, ripping apart clothes and flesh in a wet mess.

He let out a cry and fell on his side. His mind screamed about a new threat from the second car, and he forced his body to respond. He propped up on his left elbow and raised the gun. His vision blurred again, his body on fire with pain. The man in the other car exited. The two women remained. He held a small pistol. Raven shifted the .45 to the man. He wanted to fire but his trigger finger refused to respond. His vision began to fade. When the man with the small pistol fired, Raven felt his body drop, and his vision went black.

25

TOO MANY PEOPLE IN TOO SMALL AN AREA. ANOTHER NIGHT IN the Red Light District in Amsterdam's De Wallen neighborhood. It was one of three red light areas in the city. Tourists and locals alike, with diverse languages and expressions filling the air. They passed glowing red windows as they explored. Prostitutes stood behind the glass, watching, posing. It's how they attracted the attention from the mass of potential customers. Some of the windows were empty for the moment.

Bicycles lined a parking area at the end of the canal splitting one side of the street from the other. No cars allowed. The lack of vehicular access annoyed Derick Vokkert a great deal. He never went to De Wallen if he could find a way to avoid a visit.

Tonight, he had no choice.

He had a traitor to deal with, and a reputation to maintain. Vokkert dealt with turncoats personally. Always.

Vokkert cut an impressive figure in his black suit, shirt, gold tie. The tie matched his cuff links and Rolex. At the late hour of the night, not a speck of facial hair shadow covered his jaw. He was tall with dark hair, but his two large body-guards made him look smaller than his six feet. The body-guards also wore black, but neither had any gold accessories.

The three men moved at a quick pace through the mass of tourists and locals. None of the women on display distracted Vokkert. His eyes were set on a bar at the end of the street.

Alcohol wasn't allowed on the street, but smoking pot was not against the law. Vokkert's nose crinkled at the pungent stink. There was no money in soft drugs like mari-juana in Amsterdam. There was plenty of money in the hard drugs Vokkert had sold for over two decades. He didn't think too much about the conditions at home. The hard stuff was in demand not only at home but overseas, where there was plenty of money up for grabs.

Vokkert's eyes darted left and right. A few figures in the crowd stood out. The Red Light regions of Amsterdam were quite safe, and for a reason. Undercover police officers in plain clothes kept watch. They looked out for pickpockets and monitored activity in the alleys branching off from the main street. Some of them were on Vokkert's payroll. None of the return glances from the sentinels registered recogni-tion. And none of the officers hindered his movement.

Neon signs flashed in the bar's windows. The flashing colors changed the skin tones of those clustered outside. Vokkert and his men moved through the crowd and pushed their way beyond the doorway to the inside.

He walked in like he owned the place because he did. Vokkert had a stake in several Red Light establishments throughout the city. His holdings included the pornographic theater a stone's throw from a kindergarten. The school was at the end of the neighborhood. It was a great way to hook future customers, and normal in Amsterdam.

Inside, a crush of customers filled every space. It was loud from voices and juke box music, and Vokkert cringed at the American pop blaring at high volume. The stocky bartender noticed him, but his gaze went unacknowledged. Vokkert and his two guards headed for the back room.

Passing the last booths, they moved along a narrow hallway to a door. Vokkert twisted the knob. Locked. He banged a fist against the door.

"It's Vokkert! Open!" His voice was deep, powerful, menacing when he wanted. Anyone on the receiving end of his raised voice never wanted a second go-around.

The latch clicked and the door opened all the way. Joris Ditzel looked at him with his lower lip trembling.

"Surprised, Joris?"

"Derick. Yes. Usually—"

"You know in advance."

Vokkert pushed Joris out of the way. The bar manager's office wasn't small and was tastefully furnished. Desk, couch to one side, shelves and miscellaneous junk collected on the other side.

Vokkert examined Joris's narrow face and pointed nose. Joris didn't break the gaze. The bodyguards remained standing, one blocking the doorway, the other a few feet in front of Joris.

Vokkert said, "I'm disappointed."

"The bar's doing good, Derick."

"I'm not talking about the bar, Joris."

"I don't understand."

"I've been watching you dealing with the Brits on the side for six months. You've been cutting me out for *six months*, Joris."

"No! Look at the numbers—"

"I have pictures. I have *video*. You thought you were so clever. The ledgers mean nothing. You aren't talking your way out of this, Joris."

Joris lowered his eyes from Vokkert. His shoulders sank a little.

Vokkert sighed. This wasn't his favorite part of the job, but he had to do it. He had to maintain discipline in the organization.

Vokkert reached inside his jacket and withdrew a pair of thick rubber gloves. He pulled them on, careful to cover the gold Rolex on his left wrist. He watched beads of sweat form on Joris's forehead. He didn't protest any longer. Vokkert appreciated the silence.

Vokkert couldn't kill Joris, as much as he wanted to. Not at the bar any way. The police presence outside made it impossible. He'd never get out of the neighborhood without getting caught. The Amsterdam police only tolerated so much. Asking to get away with murder was too much to ask of even the most corrupt of officers.

But he could beat Joris to within an inch of his life. Then he wanted the names of his British contacts, the drug runners Joris had linked up with. When Joris finally outlived his usefulness, *then* Vokkert could properly dispose of him.

Vokkert rose from the chair.

Joris let out a squeal and tried to stand. His knees buckled. Vokkert reach him before he fell. His balled fist and arm shot forward like a piston under pressure.

Joris's head snapped back under the blow. Vokkert grabbed him before he fell on the couch and shoved him into the bodyguard behind him. The guard clamped meaty hands on Joris's shoulders and turned him to face Vokkert.

Joris made another sound and tried to struggle out of the big bodyguard's grasp. He lifted his right leg as Vokkert approached and kicked the boss in the abdomen. Vokkert yelled and doubled over. He turned away to lean against the wall a moment.

"Derick—"

Vokkert's scowl cut him off. Now he was mad. What had been a necessary task conducted with cold efficiency was now motivated by anger. Vokkert straightened and pointed a rubber-gloved finger at Joris.

"You keep making mistakes, Joris."

Vokkert moved in with both fists at his waist. He hammered Joris like a heavy bag. Hard, crushing blows to the bar manager's midsection. The bodyguard shifted his weight to keep Joris upright.

When Joris finally couldn't stay on his feet any longer, gravity pulled him from the bodyguard's grasp. He crumpled to the floor.

Vokkert stepped back, gasping from the effort. The gloves he returned to the inside of his jacket. With a silk handkerchief trimmed in gold lace, he wiped his face.

Joris struggled to breathe and didn't move. His eyes were wide, pain etched on his face.

Vokkert put the handkerchief away.

"You're lucky, Joris. Get yourself looked at. We will continue this conversation later. I want the names of your contacts and the firm who thought they could get our products cheaper."

Joris groaned. Vokkert and his bodyguards left the room.

26

THE COOL NIGHTTIME AIR DRIED THE SWEAT ON VOKKERT'S face. He and his guards went back through the crowded district the way they'd come. Vokkert wasn't thinking about Joris any longer. He'd completed the task. The night had a full agenda, and it was time to focus on the next job.

The cell phone inside his coat rang. He answered. He already knew who waited on the other end.

"Yes, sweetheart?"

The soft voice of Evelien Eulen responded.

"They're here. Waiting for you."

"I ran long."

"Are you done?"

"Yes, on my way."

"Mission accomplished?"

"Joris has been subdued, yes." He slowed his pace to be able to walk and talk at the same time.

"How hard did you hit him?"

Vokkert sighed. Evelien's obsession with violence grated on him sometimes.

"We left him drooling on the carpet, honey."

"Oh, poor Joris," she said. "I'll be waiting for you when the meeting is over. I'll wear your favorite nightie."

Which meant no nightie.

But Vokkert didn't smile or respond with enthusiasm. Work was on his mind. Work, then fun. Maybe. Sometimes work remained on his mind even when the job ended for the night, which made fun impossible.

"I'll try not to keep you waiting very long."

"Tell me, darling, did he beg?"

"Stop it."

"No, tell me."

"He kicked me."

"Not in your magic wand, I hope. Do you need me to kiss it and make it better?" She laughed.

"Fix a drink and calm down, you animal."

Evelien laughed again and hung up.

By the time Vokkert reached his car a few blocks away, he'd forgotten the conversation. He had ten men waiting for him in a conference room. They had another problem to talk about.

A problem named Branko Zupan.

DERICK VOKKERT RELAXED in the back seat of the big Mercedes. His two guards sat up front. He looked out the tinted windows at the bright lights of Amsterdam.

He'd lived in the city his whole life. He rose from a working class background to lead one of the most productive *penose* organizations in the city.

The *penose* was the Dutch equivalent to the Italian mafia but with a major difference. Instead of organized families, the *penose* were small and unaffiliated groups. No heavy infrastructure like the Italians. They operated as independent gangs with a gentleman's agreement on activity. The agreement covered territory as well. No gang was big enough to afford a major fight with another. Clashes were few, and usually ironed out through negotiations than gun fights.

Vokkert's primary focus was drugs. The Dutch crime gangs moved most of the world's ecstasy supply. Heroin and other hard narcotics supported the rest of the balance sheet. The ten men waiting for him made up the entirety of his *penose*, each with their own soldiers and enforcers. Vokkert made sure the police and politicians had appropriate payoffs. If the payoffs didn't work, they were *intimidated* into leaving them alone. Vokkert frowned on murder. It was too easy and brought heat. Disposing of somebody in such fashion required pre-planning, a place to dump the body. Murder was a last resort. Threatening a nosy cop's young child proved far more effective, in Vokkert's experience. He accomplished more with a direct conversation and a promise than with a bullet.

He accepted interference from law enforcement as a necessary part of doing business. They had a job to do, and Vokkert respected how they'd taken a side. You dance with the one who brought you. But somebody like Joris, who switched sides, was *verboten*. If Vokkert ever resorted to violence first, it was with people like Joris Ditzel. And, luckily, most of his crew stayed loyal. Once word of Joris's discipline spread, they'd remember why they were loyal.

The Mercedes slowed and turned onto the ramp for an underground garage. The building above was a skyscraper stretching into the darkness over the city. To anybody passing by, the building was the headquarters of a money management firm. It was Vokkert's private joke. The company was legit, but only served to launder Vokkert's drug money. He used a variety of legitimate businesses to move the cash.

Ten other luxury cars waited in the garage. The body-guard driving parked the car. The two big men exited but Vokkert waited a moment until they gave the all clear. Then he stepped out. Being the boss was not without risk.

A quiet elevator ride brought the trio to the top floor conference room.

Vokkert left the two guards at the door. He crossed the room to the table in the center. The lights in the room were low. Beyond the crystal clear glass making up the exterior wall, Amsterdam shined.

"Gentlemen," Vokkert said. "Thank you for being here at such a late hour."

He stopped at the head of the table and remained standing. Ten faces gazed back quietly.

"Branko Zupan is becoming a problem we can no longer ignore," he announced.

"You promised you would control him."

The speaker sat on the left side of the table, in the middle. Mr. Elo Mogensen. In charge of drug distribution for the north end of the city.

Vokkert grit his teeth. Mogensen stared at him with defiance. He wasn't alone in his thinking but he was the only one to speak.

The others turned their faces away or shifted in their seats.

Mogensen said, "We warned you Zupan was unstable."

Mogensen had a point. Vokkert couldn't argue. Zupan and his two women had come to them five years earlier. At the time, Zupan was looking for a home base. Vokkert appreciated the Croatian's understated way of carrying out violence. He wasn't a shoot-first type, either. But he had a reputation of going his own way. Some of the men seated at the table before him had objected. Vokkert had overruled them and hired Zupan and his women.

"I remember some of you did not support bringing Zupan and his crew into our group," Vokkert said. "But you cannot deny they have served us well."

Another attendee cleared his throat. Mogensen snapped his attention to a man across the table, who shook his head. Vokkert let the following silence linger a moment. Then he said, "Zupan has gone rogue. He learned of a set of photographs. They are said to be very sensitive photographs. If acquired, one might blackmail the US government into submission."

The ten men exchanged glances, as if letting out a collectively held breath.

"The pictures allegedly show the US president in a compromising position. Exact details are unknown."

Another man at the table said, "There have been rumors. The CIA—"

"Has been attempting to recover the photographs, yes. Zupan asked my permission to go after them. I said no. He went anyway."

Vokkert began to pace. He stopped to look out at the city.

Somebody said, "Did he steal any funds for this?"

"No," Vokkert said. "He used his own resources."

"We have to stop him," said Kasper Dam, who ran the group's brothels in the Red Light districts.

Vokkert turned from the glass. "He poses a great danger to our operations should he be captured. Should somebody kill him, I won't lose any sleep."

"We can't wait for anyone to do this for us," Dam said.

"Exactly. I have an idea for solving the issue."

"How much will it cost?" Mogensen again. Less aggressive than before.

"Caesar."

Another hush descended. Vokkert paced again.

"We will offer Caesar two million US to find Zupan, his women, and anybody with him. No survivors."

"We will all have to contribute to cover the expense," Dam said.

Vokkert nodded. "It's the only way to assure success. We all know Caesar's reputation. He will not fail."

The underworld only knew the man to whom Vokkert referred as Caesar, no last name. Born in Spain, Caesar operated throughout Europe as an assassin for hire. Various police and intelligence organizations wanted him for questioning. Caesar had so far eluded the global dragnet by excelling in facial disguise.

"Is there a less expensive option?" Mogensen asked.

Vokkert frowned. "Who?"

"Your girlfriend. Her associates."

"Absolutely not."

Mogensen nodded.

Vokkert checked his watch. He kept a penthouse on the top floor of the building. Evelien would be waiting for him. When she heard the news about Caesar, she too would insist he allow her to track down Branko Zupan. She had the skills and blood-lust required, but he didn't want her in danger.

"All right," Vokkert said. "Let's call it a night. I expect your money by tomorrow afternoon."

There were no further objections.

27

VOKKERT DISMISSED HIS BODYGUARDS TILL THE NEXT afternoon. He rode the elevator to the penthouse.

He stepped into the main room, sunken in the center where he had a ring of leather furniture. A glass coffee table complimented the set. The overhead lights were out. Only small plug-in nightlights provided the illumination needed to cross the bedroom.

He opened the door and closed it behind him.

"I expected you would be longer," Evelien said.

She sat up in bed, the covers turned down. She was in his favorite nightie as promised, naked with only her long black hair covering her breasts. Red lipstick matched red finger-nails. Vokkert let his eyes roam over her tanned and toned body. There were parts he stared at longer, the parts where scar tissue had left permanent marks. She'd earned them carrying out jobs for the group. In some cases, those assign-ments had turned violent.

"Are you only going to stare?"

He grinned and began getting out of his clothes.

"How was the meeting?"

"Nobody died or got mutilated beyond recognition. Why do you care?"

She laughed as he crawled onto the bed. They shared one long, lingering kiss. Vokkert broke contact to let out a groan. He rolled to the side of the bed and put his right hand under his head.

"Tonight's not a good night after all, babe. I'm beat."

"What? No. You do not deny me, darling."

She straddled him. Her long hair fell in an erotic cascade down her shoulders and back. She pushed her fingernails through his chest hair, stopping to scratch his neck. She had to lean over. Her breasts pressed into his chest. He made a grunt but still looked sleepy. She sat up and pulled her nails back toward his stomach.

He told her about the conversation with his crew and the decision he'd made to hire Caesar.

"Why not me and my girls?"

The scar across the middle of her belly where a knife had sliced through made his answer easy. "No, Evelien."

She jammed her nails into his sides. He let out a shout, snatched her wrists, and pulled her flat.

"Why?" she said, her hot breath on his face.

"This is not a negotiation."

"What is it then?" She began grinding into him. The tickle of her pubic hair was usually enough to rev his engine. Despite the long night and his desire only for sleep, the engine fired at full power.

"It's me telling you how it is and I don't want any more arguments."

"Or what?"

She was smiling as he grew harder against her.

"Or I'll put on the rubber gloves and give you the same treatment I gave Joris."

"Liar!" She bit his lower lip and he yelled again. His

surprise let her free her wrists from his grasp. She used her left hand to stay propped above him while her right seized his shaft and shoved it in. She pressed down on him, then raised upright to grind again.

This time, Vokkert didn't say no.

IF ONLY SHE had kept her mouth shut.

The assassin known only as Caesar watched the target pull out of the underground garage. She drove into the evening traffic of Berlin. He stayed back at least three car lengths, but she was easy to keep in sight. He'd cracked one of her tail lights and a spot of white stood out among the red.

The woman's death had to look like an accident. The client had been very specific. Any other method, including a staged robbery, was out of the question.

Her name was Fiona Tauscher and her fatal mistake was deciding to rat on her boss.

Caesar didn't know all the details. Knowing everything wasn't his concern. But he'd researched the client and had an idea. He was the CEO of a major pharmaceutical firm. Fiona Tauscher had an ax to grind. She wanted to talk to the German federal police, the Bundespolizei (BPOL), about her employer. The client wanted her gone. Caesar had imagined a variety of reasons she made the CEO nervous. His firm had probably produced a new vaccine which was causing sterility and/or organ damage and death. The job was worth $2 million US to Caesar. He could have stockpiled some Zyklon-B for all he cared.

He'd been watching Fiona Tauscher for three weeks to learn her routine. He was tall and trim with close-cropped hair and a chiseled face, but he never wore his original face in public. Every day a new disguise kept Fiona Tauscher from spotting him. The face he wore now looked puffy, an office worker who didn't exercise and was growing outward all around.

It was Wednesday night. He expected her to head for a bar close to the office. The previous night, Tuesday, she'd attended a yoga class. Her schedule wasn't very elaborate. Monday: home. Tuesday: yoga. Wednesday: drinks with friends. Thursday and Friday at home. Weekends varied too much to bother with. He didn't see her mix with many men. She was short and thick in the middle with dark hair. Her routine might vary a little now and then, but by week two he could intercept her at several points. He could now figure out how to get rid of her.

Caesar had created several scenarios and scouted her apartment during his surveillance. He had a good idea of how to stage her accidental demise.

Too much wine was bad for you.

Now it was only a matter of precise timing.

They drove two blocks but Fiona Tauscher passed the bar at which she normally stopped. Caesar's pulse quickened. She was breaking routine. Okay. Fine. A delay. He'd have to watch what she did instead and see if the change required an adjustment to his plan.

He followed her to a restaurant and parked a few spaces down from her car. She entered the restaurant alone. He waited a bit longer and went in after her. Might as well get dinner while he watched her.

He sat alone in the dining room at a corner table. Fiona Tauscher sat with a man at a table in the center of the dining room.

Having missed how she greeted him, Caesar wasn't sure if she had a date, or if she was dining with a rep from BPOL. They talked informally, each quite animated; not simply a date, but a first date. Both Fiona Tauscher and her new friend made sure their best smiles were front and center.

Caesar buttered a slice of sour dough bread a waiter had placed on the table. Poor little bitch. She had to go shooting her mouth off and be a superhero. For what? She'd gained nothing in the end and put a target on her back. A nice big target. She might have hopes and dreams, but Caesar wasn't bothered about those. He had a job to do. The client expected results.

Make it look like an accident.

Judging by how fast she drank her glass of red wine, she was going to make it easy. She asked their waiter for another glass before they ordered their meals.

28

SHE BURPED AS SHE CLIMBED THE STEPS.

Caesar waited in an alcove off the third-floor landing of the apartment complex. Each door opened on an exposed walkway with only a rail providing fall protection. The exposed floors encircled a center courtyard.

No elevators. Residents on the upper floors had to climb a long set of steps, which let off at each floor before continuing upward. A great workout. The way Fiona Tauscher took the steps in heels, she was used to the climb. He bet her legs and rear end looked great from the effort.

She cleared the last step and put one foot on the lacing. As she lifted her foot, Caesar stepped out of the alcove. She sucked in a startled breath, and began to say excuse me, but never finished. Caesar shoved. Fiona Tauscher screamed and fell back. The screams stopped as she tumbled back down the steps to the courtyard. She sprawled on the concrete, her head bent at the neck and leaking red, legs twisted in opposite directions, arms flung wide.

Caesar didn't yell an alarm. He knew the layout of the building well. He followed the walkway to the other side and hurried down another flight of steps. On the other side, the floors faced a street and overlooked the parking lot. He'd left his car close by.

His heart was racing a little as he drove away. He felt hot. Cracking a window, he let the cool night air into the car.

Caesar drove back to his hotel. During the drive he phoned his client. The client didn't answer, but the assassin only needed to leave a short message.

"It's done."

He ended the call. Once the police reported the "accident" the client would have his confirmation. Her blood alcohol level would point to the cause of her slip-and-fall. Caesar didn't take pictures. Make the kill, get out of the area. He spent only enough time in the hotel room to grab two already packed suitcases. Had he aborted the hit, he'd have stayed another night. Fiona Tauscher and her date had left the restaurant in separate cars, going in different directions, after parting without a kiss. Caesar had seen no reason to abort as long as he reached the apartment before the target arrived.

Now it was time to go.

On the road again, Caesar made another call. He had a jet on stand-by at Berlin Brandenburg Airport. The pilot responded to his request to prepare for take-off with a promise all would be ready when he arrived. The jet was waiting for him at a private hanger.

Regular flights were not an option for him. His disguises might be good, but they were not foolproof. He feared advancements in facial recognition might someday render the effects moot. It was only a matter of time before the technology became smart enough to see his real face regardless.

Private flights were safer.

For now.

Caesar had no doubt his time was ending. Soon there'd be

no way to hide at all. He needed more money before he'd feel comfortable hanging up his guns. And he needed something to ensure protection because even retired he'd still be a wanted man.

The money would be the easy part.

The other? Maybe only a dream.

The jet took off fifteen minutes after he arrived. Once the pilots reached cruising altitude, Caesar left his seat and stepped into the lavatory. He turned on the light but left the door open.

He removed his hair piece. The bushy curls he dropped on the floor leaving close-cropped dark hair, bald on top, in its place.

He soaked a wash cloth with hot water and scrubbed his face. The tan he'd applied vanished. He pulled off the rubber strips used to change the shape of his jaw and cheeks, and the stray adhesive left behind. Another scrub. He dried his face and examined his own countenance in the mirror.

He never saw his own face enough. It wasn't like the old days when he killed for a cause and he wanted the enemy to know his face and his name.

But he'd been younger then. Now he killed only for money. The cause had died ages ago. He wasn't the type to join another which would fail as surely as the other.

He could keep his own face during the flight. By the time they landed at Orly in Paris, he'd need yet another face. He had a supply of make-up and disguise kits on the plane.

He had enough time to sit with a drink and watch the scenery below. He could forget work for a while.

CAESAR PUT his previous face back on so it matched his passport. Customs cleared him without incident.

He used Paris as his base of operations, and one of his associates met him. He had several such associates in Paris. They acted his defense against potential danger. They screened clients and set up appointments, and made sure appointments weren't traps by American or British agents. The operative's name was Alexia Devereux. She was younger than him. Tall with wide hips and long black hair, she was a nice sight to see after a busy trip. Her rich brown eyes stood out the most against her pale white face. Unlike most women in France, she didn't care for sunbathing, at the beach or anywhere else.

They drove to an apartment in the Eighth District near the Champs Elysees. The expense of the area kept the population small. Caesar felt comfortable as long as he remained in the district's confines.

Alexia slid the car into the ground floor garage. She followed behind him up an indoor stairwell to the apartment on floor up. A door led them into the living room. Caesar pulled off his wig again and said, "Thanks for the lift."

Alexia took a cell phone from her purse. "We should talk about a note I received from the Netherlands."

"Wait." Caesar removed his disguise in the bathroom, then rejoined Alexia. The operative sat on the couch. Caesar grabbed a bottle of beer from the refrigerator and sat at the counter across from the couch.

"Now. Tell me."

"Derick Vokkert, Dutch gangster in Amsterdam. He'd like to see you about a personnel problem."

"Tell him to come here. I'm not going to Amsterdam."

Alexia tapped a finger on the phone screen to send the reply.

"How did Berlin go?" she asked.

"Fine," Caesar said. He swallowed more beer. He liked the apartment but always felt like he was returning to a prison cell. The small space didn't defeat the feeling. He told Alexia to leave and let him know when the Dutchman answered his reply.

He sat in the empty space once the woman departed. What did he really have? A full bank account, but nowhere to enjoy the money. At some point, the cash lost meaning. What he needed was freedom.

VOKKERT ACCEPTED the terms and met Caesar two days later. The meeting lasted less than thirty minutes as Vokkert outlined the problem. He showed pictures of Branko Zupan and his female companions, the Lovrekovic sisters. He also gave Caesar a list of people and places to begin his search.

Caesar agreed to the job with half of the two million US transferred to his account by the end of the day. Vokkert said no problem.

During the drive back to the hotel, Evelien Eulen once again tried to change her lover's mind.

"I would cost you nothing but expenses," she said.

She sat on the passenger side of the back seat, legs crossed, watching Vokkert stare out the window. The driver navigated traffic with ease.

"We settled this."

"It's only a reminder."

"There's more information I've received over the last 48 hours," he said. "The information confirms why we need Caesar, and why I'm not putting you at risk."

"What?"

"Zupan's trio of gunmen."

"Shaw and—" she paused.

"I forget, too," Vokkert said. "But all three are dead."

"What happened?"

"Whatever Zupan has begun is bringing out unknown talent."

"You don't need Caesar if somebody is already on the trail."

"Not a chance I'm willing to take," Vokkert said.

"Blah, blah," Evelien said. "Do you think the clues you gave Caesar will help him?"

"They better. We're grasping at straws the way Zupan moves around."

"Where were the gunmen killed?"

"One in Barcelona, other two in Ireland. City called Wexford."

"Want to know what I'd do if you put me on the job?"

"Shut your mouth, sweetie."

"Why don't you put something in it, darling?"

"Not in the car, Evelien."

"You're no fun."

Vokkert admitted it was one of his flaws.

29

PAIN FILLED EVERY SENSE. EVEN ONES SAM RAVEN WASN'T aware existed.

He awoke slowly, his pulse quickening as he began taking stock of his surroundings. Small room. Soft bed. Plain decorations. Random trinkets on the shelves and white walls. He couldn't make out all the shapes with his blurred vision. He wiped his eyes but it didn't help. He was in the guest room of a house. Whose house? What was on his chest? He was bare from the waist up. Somebody had shaved squares of chest hair to accommodate taped sensors. The sensors held down wires leading to the right side of the bed. Heart monitor. EKG machine. Somebody had plugged an IV drip into his right arm as well. The IV tower stood between the heart monitor and EKG.

Red welts and bandaged cuts covered his chest. His head hurt. He felt the side of his face. His skin was sensitive. Further up at his right temple, another bandage covered a square of space. A patch of his hair had been shaved to make room for the bandage.

Raven shouted, "Hey!" His voice sounded hoarse. "Hey!"

Louder. He started breathing harder. He tried to sit up but it hurt too much. With a grunt of defeat, he lay flat again. *Where am I? What happened? Where's Megan?*

Ana Gray sat at a large oak desk in front of a wide computer screen.

She had a variety of documents open on the wide screen. The documents were reports from her agents around the world. Not all of the information was actionable. A new jihadist group forming was something to watch. She'd offer the info to the CIA, MI6, or Mossad once she confirmed the group was active. She also wanted the names of the members. She sent a note to the operative who dug up the information to keep tabs on the players.

Another report concerned human trafficking, a matter she kept an eye on most days. She sent the report, gratis, to a group of former commandos. They had taken up the cause of fighting that particular enemy. She'd sent them money in the past and facilitated delivery of small arms. They wouldn't refuse the information.

More information of similar content filled the screen. She scanned most of the documents fast. Most of the data she filed away for attention later; others for further review straight away.

"Hey!"

The yell startled her. Raven had been asleep for 72 hours. Despite what the doctor had said, she'd feared he might not wake up. Now he *was* awake, a good sign. He was probably confused. He would want to know where he was and what happened to bring him back to Barcelona.

He yelled again as she left her desk to head for the stairs.

Raven tensed as the door opened. Ana Gray stood in the doorway. She stepped into the room and closed the door. She wore her usual slacks and blouse and diamond necklace. He noted she wore white slippers and wanted to smile but had no power to make the expression.

"You're awake."

"How the hell did I get here?"

Ana Gray sat on the edge of the bed. Her face showed concern, her mouth a straight line. Raven remained on his back. He wasn't sure he could sit up if he wanted to and wasn't going to try again.

"I didn't tell you the truth," she said.

"Tell me now."

"I had two of my men watching you. Who was the woman?"

"I didn't tell you the truth, either. It was Megan."

"Then we're even. I told them not to intervene. I changed the order after the accident."

"Uh-huh."

"Medics took you to the hospital. My men went in posing as MI5 and claimed you were a suspect wanted for questioning. They took you from the hospital and brought you here. My personal physician has been looking at you twice a day."

"Only me?"

"Yes, Sam."

"Where's Megan?"

Ana Gray looked sad.

"Where is she, Ana?"

"She's gone, Sam."

Raven let out a sound and a pain in his chest joined the rest of the hurt. His mind flashed back to the moments before the crash. He saw the bullets hit Megan, saw her body fall. Once the air bags went off, he had no visual memory of what happened next. But he remembered getting out of the car. He remembered the face of the man who shot him.

"She was dead when the police pulled her out of the car," Ana continued.

Raven's vision blurred again. This time with tears.

"I'm sorry, Sam."

Raven wiped his eyes. "Where was I shot? Side of the head?"

"The bullet grazed you. Took out a chunk of skin, though."

"The stuff in the car. Our bags."

"Stolen. There was nothing for the police to find."

"Then whoever shot us has the pictures, Ana."

"Sam—"

"I gotta get out of this bed."

Raven attempted to sit up again. He felt the wires pulling at his skin as he moved. But another wave of pain accompanied with dizziness forced him down again. He lay gasping. He tried to move his legs, but they didn't respond. He wiggled his toes. Everything worked but he'd been on his back too long.

"You're not ready, Sam."

He opened his mouth to argue but nothing came out. She was right. He had to recover before continuing the fight.

"The wreck banged you up. You need to rest."

"I need to get even. I saw the face of the man who shot me."

"Not yet."

"When?"

"My doctor will be here again in a few hours. You can ask him."

She rose and went to the door.

"Ana?"

She turned. "What, Sam?"

"Thanks."

"I should have told my men to do something."

"And I should have trusted you."

"We were both wrong."

She went out. The door clicked closed.

Raven stared at the ceiling and hurt more than physically. They were both wrong, yeah. And he lost his chance to see if he might be able to live with somebody again. He'd go after the enemy alone.

Always alone.

30

Branko Zupan had no intention of losing sight of the quarry.

Getting his hands on the pictures would be the win of a lifetime.

He swung in and out of lanes, following the SUV as his gunners fired on the car driven by Raven and Megan. The two women with him remained quiet, focused, as he steered. The target car finally veered off the road and overturned. Zupan crossed two lanes to get to the right shoulder. He stopped behind the wreck.

Raven, on his knees, fired on the two gunners from the SUV. He couldn't save his men, but it didn't matter. He took out his gun. As if on cue, the two women brought out their pistols. They handled the guns with familiarity and ease. They'd been using guns for attack and defense since they were teenagers.

"Stay in the car," Zupan told the women. He left and walked around the front. He was slightly less than six feet, but well-muscled. His full head of hair had once been black; now, it featured flecks of gray. His face showed constant strain. Fighting for one's life from an early age had left its mark.

Raven swung toward Zupan with his gun up. Zupan didn't flinch. He fired once. A spray of blood erupted from the right side of Raven's head. Zupan grinned. The man who had been a thorn in the side of the underworld for so long pitched forward and landed on his face. He did not move again. *Exit Raven.*

"Hurry," the tall woman said.

Zupan pivoted left. He approached Raven's car. The two women left the car. The tall one joined him. The shorter woman jumped behind the wheel.

"Hurry," the tall woman said.

Zupan and the tall woman reached Raven's car. The woman checked inside. Nothing but the dead woman and she said so. Zupan shot the lock off the trunk and shoved the lid open. They didn't have time to sort the gear bags. Zupan grabbed one and the woman grabbed the other.

Both ran back to the car. Zupan climbed into the back seat with both bags. The tall woman dropped into the front passenger seat.

"Go!" the tall woman shouted.

Her sister floored the pedal and gouged the dirt and grass beneath the tires. The car screeched when the rubber met the blacktop. They sped ahead of the pack of slow traffic. Other drivers slowed to see the wreck off the shoulder.

Zupan let the girls deal with the getaway. Like a five-year-old on Christmas morning, he tore through the gear bags. Clothes didn't matter. Ammo, ditto. He tossed a lockbox on the floor of the car. He didn't care. He didn't stop until he found the envelope of pictures. He'd been looking for them since first learning of their existence. He grasped the envelope and yanked it out of the back.

Opening the flap, Zupan looked inside. The pictures were

there. He removed them and examined each shot. He jostled in the seat as the car hit bumps and made sharp turns. None of it mattered and did not tear his attention away from the prize. He had the pictures. His grin widened as he shuffled through each.

Finally, he had freedom in his hands.

"Are they good?"

Zupan glanced over the top edge of one photo. The tall woman in the passenger seat had twisted around to look at him.

Branko Zupan handed the pictures to Jasna Lovrekovic. She was black-haired with fiery eyes. She stood an inch taller than Zupan but he didn't care. Jasna Lovrekovic was a stunner. He'd fallen in love with her upon their first meeting at age fifteen.

Jasna let out a laugh. "It's geezer porn! An old man screwing a potato." She turned to her sister. Petra remained stoic behind the wheel. Zupan never expected Petra Lovrekovic to show any emotion. She never did. The trio had collected many mental and physical scars over the years. Petra had the most. She was five years younger than Jasna.

Jasna handed back the pictures. Zupan returned them to the envelope.

"Nobody wants to look at something gross like that," Jasna said. "He's old and the woman is fat."

"Doesn't matter," Zupan said.

They had the pictures. Raven and Megan were out of the way.

They had to get out of Ireland and to their hideout in Wales. But it was a long way to the hideout. No flights for the three of them either. They'd travel via smuggling routes all the way to the UK.

Eyes open the whole way. Anybody they encountered might be a threat.

Forever vigilant. The motto Branko Zupan lived by.

He'd learned the hard way during what was now called the Homeland War. The Croatian War of Independence. For Zupan, the war didn't need a name. It had only been an ordeal to survive. He and Jasna and Petra *had* survived. And now they had the pictures. Their future survival was now a guarantee. As long as they reached Wales in one piece.

Petra kept driving. Zupan allowed himself a deep, satisfied breath.

Almost home free.

First priority: *Ditch the car.* Petra took an exit and whipped the car along several blocks, with a few sharp turns, until she stopped in an alley. The trio piled out. Zupan carried the gear bags. They jumped into another car placed there earlier. Jasna took the wheel this time. Petra rode shotgun and Zupan climbed in back with the bags again.

Jasna drove out of the alley and found her way to a motorway on-ramp. They were heading north out of Wexford to Dublin. From there they'd pick up a boat and cross the Irish sea to the coast of Wales. Another drive to their final destination, and then a few days of rest. They never stayed in place long. Zupan made a sport of moving from one safe house to another.

Jasna trusted Branko's plan and arrangement. But she and Petra had been through too much to relax their vigilance.

Jasna turned to Petra. The younger woman brushed her hair behind her ears. She looked straight ahead, but her gaze was far away.

"Ready to go home?"

"Such as it is," Petra said. Her expression remained stoic.

Jasna faced forward and continued driving.

She'd been taking care of her sister for a long time. Since their parents died at the start of Croatia's so-called Homeland War.

31

1991. VOKAVAR, CROATIA. THE SHELLING BEGAN IN AUGUST and the fighting soon after. Serbian soldiers entered the city and began a street-to-street slaughter of Croats. Thousands had died during the shelling; thousands more had already fled the city. Those who stayed behind lived under a tremendous mental strain. A strain caused by falling bombs and the crackle of gunfire in the middle of the night.

Vulnerable families cowered within the rubble of their bomb-smashed homes. They prayed the onslaught would spare them. But the city fell. Serbs advanced for the final takeover. Any hope they had of escaping alive dwindled.

The Lovrekovic family refused to give up their farm. The father did not want to give up land his family had held for five generations. When Serb troops finally arrived, the two brothers braced for a fight. They had bolt-action rifles. But they were no match for the battle-hardened pirates who demanded their surrender at the point of automatic weapons.

Jasna remembered how the conflict began very well.

Croatia wanted to break away from the Yugoslav Republic after the fall of the Soviet Union. Serbia didn't want to let the territory go, and instead keep Yugoslavia together as it had been under Tito. Keeping the country as one would restrain the various ethnic groups within from tearing each other apart. Croatia's move threatened Serbians within Croatia, and Serbia responded with force. The violence came after months of simmering conflict between the politicians and the public.

Jasna also remembered the last time she saw her father. He and her uncle convinced the family to stay on the farm, and not join the flood of refugees fleeing the city. Jasna and her ten-year-old sister Petra were too young to argue. They clung close to their mother and aunts as the men did their best to fortify the property. But when the moment of truth came, the Lovrekovic men died at the hands of Serbs who knew how to fight better.

She'd burned the last image of her father into her memory. He was standing beside his dead brother, firing his rifle. The return salvo from a Serb seemed louder than anything she ever heard. Then she saw him fall.

The bullets seemed to hit her father in slow motion. Two in the lower abdomen, a third ripped through his stomach. The last two rounds split open his chest. It was like watching the bullets climb a ladder to her father's heart.

Her mother and aunt rushed Jasna and Peta into the basement. They tried to hide, but soon the voices of soldiers broke through the haze of shock. The troops demanded they come out. "We won't hurt you!" they called. The women didn't answer. They couldn't talk if they wanted to. They held each other close. The only sounds they uttered consisted of panicked whimpers.

The Serbs entered the basement, a line of big, sweaty

soldiers carrying Kalashnikovs. They seized the women and dragged them upstairs and outside, forcing them to hands and knees in a garden. Jasna felt her heart beating in her throat. Her legs wouldn't work. She clutched at her kid sister the way her mother ordered, but soon it didn't matter. The soldiers forced the girls apart and held them to one side. The men took turns raping their mother and aunt before shooting both. The men then turned their attention to the young girls.

Jasna remembered trying to scream. She screamed only in her mind. Nothing escaped her throat. The first man grabbed her.

And his face popped like a balloon.

More gunfire erupted and Jasna grabbed for Petra, covering her sister with her body. The Serbs received some of their own medicine. Bullets cut through them where they stood. None of the soldiers managed to get a shot off at the new arrivals. The garden had once been a special place for the girls. It was where their mother taught them how to grow food. Now it was a graveyard.

The shooting stopped. Dead Serbs, and their mother and aunt, littered the ground. A new group of men led by a skinny teenager reached for them. Jasna took a gulp of air. She recognized the boy. He was Branko Zupan. His family lived two miles away on another farm. They knew each other from school. He and his crew whisked them away from the farm and the girls didn't look back. Branko explained he and his crew were sweeping through the area to kill Serbs. They'd heard the shooting from the farm and ran to help. He was sorry they were too late. Jasna and her sister had nothing else to do but run off with them. With a crying Petra clutching close, Jasna followed Zupan and his group to a hideout. They didn't stay long, finally joining the flow of refugees. Neither had any idea what fate had in store for them.

They ran from one place to another till the end of the war. Never safe, always under fire, but growing defiant in the chaos. Jasna and Petra learned to fight and killed with as much efficiency as expert commandos. They were only fighting to protect each other and their temporary shelter. By the end of the war, there was nothing to go back to. They were a family, a family of choice, but one nonetheless. They carried on by surviving by any means possible.

But it was not without cost. While romantic feelings had blossomed between Jasna and Zupan, Petra was left out in the cold. The war affected her the most. Her stoic attitude, lack of communication, and dependence on her sister betrayed the inner scars the three of them worked very hard to conceal. Petra was good in a fight. She knew how to steal. She knew how to manipulate others to get what she wanted. But Jasna also knew Petra was the most damaged of them all. Worse, she didn't know how to make her better. She wasn't sure it was possible to make her better.

But as Jasna drove north to Dublin, Zupan in the back and Petra in the seat beside her, she knew he was right. The contents of the pictures did not matter, as disgusting as they were. The pictures held the key to carving out, finally, their own slice of the world. One where nobody would hunt them or bother them. They might finally know what peace looked like. Maybe she and Petra, in honor of their parents, could start a new garden, and replace sad memories with new ones.

At least she could dream about doing so. She wasn't sure it was possible. Their life had left her cynical and untrusting of everybody but Petra and Zupan. She knew the other two felt likewise.

But for now, they had a chance. They were a family. They

would conquer the future or die together. There was no in-between, no room for compromise.

Jasna drove on. They had a ninety-minute drive to Dublin, and then a boat ride to the UK. She had no plans to let down her guard in the meantime.

32

THEY REACHED DUBLIN PORT AND PARKED THE CAR. THE ferry to Wales didn't leave till morning, but they were in a hurry. Zupan saw no reason to wait while he had precious cargo in hand. He found the boat they'd hired at one of the private slips, and the sisters followed him aboard.

The craft was a large fishing boat, zero accommodations, but the trio wasn't interested in comfort. They crowded the corner bench seat at the stern, with only a flimsy canopy supported by metal bars above. The boat left the port for the crossing of the Irish Sea. Destination: Wales. They had a house on the coast overlooking the ocean. Quiet, isolated, with plenty of open ground to watch for attackers.

Zupan leaned back on the bench seat. He held his arms over the two gear bags on either side of him. Jasna sat on his left, Petra his right.

The chug of the motor filled the night. Diesel fumes trickled Zupan's nose and he winced at the stink. If the smell bothered the women, they made no mention. He remembered the times they'd smelled worse scents than diesel fumes.

Water lapped at the hull. He could hear the water, but it was too dark to see. Black surrounded them. The boat's running lights made the sensation of traveling through a dark void more than intense.

Jasna leaned close to his ear. "Can we trust them?" She motioned her head at the boat's operators.

Three men, all husky and bulky, ran the boat with the precision of habitual sailors. One steered and navigated; the other two used night-vision goggles to scan the water. Every few minutes one of the two broke away to tend to another task.

Zupan had only dealt with the captain who manned the helm. He told Jasna.

"Can you *trust* him?" she said again.

"I've paid him. But, no, I don't. All he's had to do in the time between taking the job and now is ask around about what we might be doing."

"If he knows about the pictures—"

Petra finally spoke up. "Stop. We need to get some sleep. You two go ahead and I'll keep watch awhile."

"It's a good idea," Zupan told Jasna.

She agreed and shifted to lean on Zupan's shoulder.

The chugging engine lulled them to sleep.

Petra wanted them sleeping so she could vomit.

She stood, brushing back the flap of her jacket. She pulled her pistol from the inside-the-waistband holster over her right hip. The compact SIG-Sauer P-228 nine-millimeter hid well as she pressed it close to her thigh. She watched the boat's crew out the left corner of her eye as she stood at the stern. She stared into the dark a moment. Her stomach felt funny. Waves of discomfort hit in regular intervals. It was only a matter of time before she'd bend over the side and throw up into the water. She hated boats. She hated being on a boat. But Branko said it was the only way. She'd pointed out they could fly home as they had flown to Ireland, but he nixed the idea. The boat was safer, he said, more clandestine. She was growing tired of their never-ending cloak-and-dagger lifestyle. She'd known nothing else since her parents died, but deep down she knew there was a better way to live.

None of them were getting younger. A life on the run was a young person's game, and they didn't qualify any longer. If they didn't make a change soon, their enemies would pick them off like wounded animals in the forest.

She gripped the hand rail on top of the gunwale. A glance behind her showed the boat crew still busy. A red light flashed atop the masthead. The captain shouted something to his men and they replied. She faced the water again. If she could see the horizon, it might settle her stomach. The trick had worked before. But only darkness stretched before her. She was staring into nothing. Her stomach turned over again and she groaned.

She clutched the SIG nine-millimeter tight and leaned over the back, vomiting into the churn of water kicked up by the twin engines below the bow line. She coughed and retched and waited for the moment to pass. She stopped as panic gripped her. A foot scraped the deck behind her. She spun, a little unsteady, and raised the gun in one motion. The startled face of one of the crew, minus his night-vision goggles, didn't stop her. She put pressure on the trigger.

The man put up his hands. "Whoa! Steady! I have sea sick pills if you want one."

"Go away," Petra said. She let off the trigger but didn't remove her finger. She wasn't going to let anybody get close to Jasna and Zupan or the gear bags. "Go back to your duties and leave us alone."

"Okay," the man said, taking a step back. He kept an eye on her as she maintained her sight picture. The man's nose was dead bang in the SIG's night sights. She'd push his nose through the back of his head with a hollow-point slug if he tried anything. He finally turned and resumed his place on the port side. She heard him say something to the other crew member. The words faded in the rushing wind before they reached her. The captain remained contained in the wheelhouse, unaware of the drama no more than ten feet behind them.

Petra spit into the ocean. Her mouth tasted awful. She needed mouthwash or a shot of whiskey. She lowered her pistol but did not return the handgun to her holster. She'd keep it close until it was her turn to sleep, and then she wouldn't sleep very hard at all.

Jasna and Zupan were out cold. Jasna was snoring. How she could snore loud enough to overpower the engine and wind Petra didn't know. Her sister had always snored with the volume of a freight train tooting its horn through a narrow tunnel.

She paced the deck, but the view did not change. She sat to face the wheelhouse and the forward direction of the boat. *How much longer?* She wanted to be back on solid ground as fast as possible.

She also wanted to be busy again. Inactivity made her think, and when Petra let her thoughts wander, she ended up sad. Every time. She was still a little girl trapped in a basement with men coming down the steps to rape her. No matter how old she was, no matter how many similar men she'd killed, the fear never left her. She wondered if she'd ever shake the memories. She wondered if the experience had damaged her beyond repair. And she was afraid to talk to Jasna and Zupan about how she felt because she didn't want them to think she was getting soft. She didn't want them to lose faith in her.

She'd already lost faith in herself.

33

ZUPAN SNAPPED AWAKE AT PETRA'S NUDGE.

"Time to switch," she said.

Jasna awoke too and yawned and stretched as Zupan stood. They were traveling faster now, the wind blowing harder. The water churned around the boat as it sliced through.

"Okay," Zupan said.

Petra sat. She and her sister curled up. Jasna dozed off again and Petra soon after.

Zupan stood alone on the deck and looked forward. The chilly wind tinged with salt water spray stabbed at his face. He went to the ladder ahead and climbed to the wheelhouse. The captain stood at the helm in warm comfort.

"Nice and toasty in here," Zupan said.

"Running the boat has its privileges," the captain said. He glanced at Zupan and for the first time the Croatian mercenary noticed the man's bulbous nose.

"Boxer?"

"What?"

"You a boxer?"

"For a while. My nose?"

"Looks like you've taken a hit or two, yeah."

"Too many hits."

Zupan watched the artificial horizon on the GPS screen. There were lights ahead, lining the true horizon, but they weren't close enough to identify any of the land mass yet.

Zupan had never stayed in one place more than a few days. For this current situation, remaining in Wales for an extended length would serve their purposes. A part of him wasn't 100% convinced of the plan, so he'd keep the decision fluid in case the situation changed. But for now, he planned to stay put. He'd pick an appropriate time to inform the American government of the stranglehold he'd soon have on the current president.

He had to be careful, though. The hold would only work as long as the sitting president remained in office. Once he was out, it would be open season again. Zupan had to come up with a way to remain in safe confines once the "protection" outlived its usefulness. But he expected to have plenty of time to make the arrangements.

All he needed was enough time. There was never enough time.

"How much longer?" he asked the captain.

The captain consulted the electronic nav screen on his console. "Another two hours till we hit South Stack and then a swing around to Holyhead. Quick and easy."

"Okay."

Zupan climbed down the ladder to the wet and cold deck and resumed his vigilance. Jasna and Petra remained asleep.

The boat pulled in at the Holyhead Marina without incident. Bright lights lit the marina, but at the late hour, nobody loitered to see them arrive. Zupan and the Lovrekovic sisters bid farewell to the captain and his crew. They off-boarded with the stolen gear bags. The captain told his men to break out the reserve fuel containers and top off the boat for the return voyage. The men were out of Zupan's mind as soon as his feet hit the jetty.

Zupan's local associates, Milos and Klaus, met them with a running van. The heater, blasting, was a relief after the overnight chill. Petra was the last to climb inside and she pulled the side door shut. Milos drove away.

Zupan said, "Is the place ready?"

Klaus, a perpetually scruffy man but a good gunman, turned in the passenger seat. He looked at Zupan. The glare from the dashboard lights only lit one side of his face.

"It's ready, Branko. I'm not sure you want to go there, though. I have another—"

"Wait. What's the problem?"

"Somebody's looking for you."

Zupan grunted. "Took him long enough."

"I heard from some of our friends back home. They told me Vokkert has sent somebody."

"Who did he hire?"

"Caesar."

Zupan cursed. Jasna and Petra looked at him with wide eyes. Zupan only said, "Caesar I did not expect."

"Who did you expect?" Jasna said.

"Evelien."

Klaus spoke again. "I took the liberty of securing—"

Zupan waved him off. "No. Our original spot is fine."

"Branko—" Jasna began.

"Stop. If Derick had sent somebody else, we would follow Klaus's backup suggestion. Caesar doesn't worry me."

"Why?"

"I know him better than he knows himself. Let him come. If he doesn't listen to reason, the world will be less one expert assassin."

"You're risking us all, Branko."

"No, I'm not."

"How can you be so sure?"

"We all come from the same mold, Jasna. We all want the same thing. I'll be able to offer Caesar what he's never found for himself."

"We need to run," Jasna said.

"The whole point of going to Ireland was to fix it so we won't have to run anymore," Zupan said. "I'm not reverting to old habits because you're getting nervous."

"I'm not nervous."

"Then you can prove it by trusting me. Have I ever let you down before?"

Jasna stared at him.

"Have I?" Zupan asked her again.

"No."

"And I'm not going to let you down this time. What do you think, Petra?"

"I just want this over," the younger woman said. "So whatever."

"We'll have our answer in a few days, I'm sure," Zupan said.

Jasna shifted in her seat. Milos drove through the night.

THE HIDEOUT OVERLOOKING the ocean had plenty of wide, defensible space. They had trees and boulders to contend with, but nothing Zupan wasn't confident they could handle if anybody came snooping. Zupan surveyed the terrain from the porch. Milos and Klaus stood near him. Jasna and Petra were already inside. Zupan approved and told his gunners so.

Klaus, the stockier of the pair, who had said nothing during the pick up and drive to the hideout, finally spoke.

"Do you want to see the weapons we collected?"

Zupan shook his head. "I'm sure it's enough. We can review everything tomorrow."

"We found a good escape route as well," Klaus added.

Zupan shook his head. "Tomorrow. We all need some rest."

A cool breeze picked up, chilling the coat-less Zupan. He took the cue and went inside, followed by the two gunmen. Milos locked and bolted the door behind him.

———

PETRA LOVREKOVIC STARED at her bed. It would be the first bed she slept in since the Wexford adventure began. She wasn't sure what to do. She'd reached the point mentally where the basics escaped her. A lifetime of running, surviving, and trying to stay one step ahead caused her to think longer than necessary. Zupan claimed they were safe now. She wasn't sure. Not with the news of the assassin Caesar on their trail.

"Hey."

Petra turned. Jasna stood in the doorway.

"Like the room?"

"It's small," Petra said. "But it's fine." She added, "This whole place is small. We'll be bumping into each other all the time."

"At least there are two bathrooms."

"Sure."

"What's the matter?"

"The two people in Ireland."

"What about them?"

"What if they have friends who come after us? We got this Caesar guy, and whoever else wants our heads."

"Well, whatever security we have here will be short-lived then."

"I'm getting tired of the killing, Jasna."

"It's the way it is. For now. With these pictures Branko can finally get us to a place—"

"It's a crazy idea and you know it. It's not going to stop the Americans from coming after us. Everybody is going crazy about these pictures and it's blinding them to reality. This isn't ever going to stop. We're always going to be running."

"Go to bed, Petra. You'll feel better in the morning."

Jasna pulled the door closed and Petra stood alone. She sat on the edge of the bed. At least it was soft. The killing had gone on too long, and she wasn't sure how much more she could take. There had simply been too much, from as far back as the war until now. And neither Jasna nor Zupan ever took her feelings into account.

What could they realistically do? What did she expect? Jasna and Zupan had the same experience as her. They didn't know any other way of life.

But maybe Jasna had a point. Petra undressed and found a bathrobe in her bag. It was warm and frayed at the edges, but still comfortable, and gave her a sense of normalcy. She'd lost so much over the course of her life it was nice to have kept hold of something as simple as a bathrobe. Grabbing her toothbrush and paste, she cleaned her teeth in the bathroom and then climbed into bed. She didn't think she'd sleep much but didn't have long to think. She dropped off within a few minutes.

34

ZAGREB. IT WASN'T CAESAR'S FIRST VISIT, AND AFTER HE WAS through it might be a long time before he returned. He didn't intend to come and go quietly.

Caesar had always liked Zagreb, especially when the weather was good. And the weather looked terrific as he stepped out of his hotel and onto the sidewalk. Clear blue sky, mountains north of the city a bright green. Rebuilding after the Homeland War had restored most of the city, but scars remained. Memorials, murals, all dedicated to the thousands of Croats who perished in the war for independence.

He'd been in Zagreb for two days, scouting the leads provided by Vokkert. Branko Zupan had many connections, mostly those in the underground criminal fraternity. Caesar had a plan for dealing with them. The war might have been long past, but he planned to bring back the scorched earth of the conflict, but on a minor scale. Nobody would weep over the bodies he might have to leave behind if they didn't cooperate.

He walked for two blocks to get some air in his lungs and

work out the kinks in his body. When he was ready, he hailed a passing cab, and asked for an address. The cab dropped him off as requested. Caesar did not enter the coffee shop at the address he'd provided. He left the cab and walked another two blocks to a hotel with a red roof. Red roofs were a motif in the neighborhood, and the Hotel St. Clare was no exception. The hotel was small, three stories. The primary business of the establishment wasn't rooms for visiting tourists. One could book a room and enjoy a nice stay at a very cozy location, but there was a dark side to the coziness, and the proprietor went to great lengths to conceal the true business from his guests. The real business of the hotel happened in the back room, and at various undisclosed locations throughout the city.

The hotel was a front for a profitable gun running operation controlled by Jakov Perusko. Franco wasn't up to date on Perusko's background. To him, it didn't matter how long the gun operation had been running. What he cared about was Perusko's connection to Branko Zupan. Caesar wanted to know where to find Zupan. If Perusko refused to provide, there would be consequences. He wasn't Caesar's only lead, but he was a good place to start.

Caesar walked up the steps of the white building to the front door. He went inside, paused to admire the rustic lobby, built using various shades of wood. The furniture was also made up of darker colors. Usual big screen television, showing a cable news channel, occupied a spot in the bar left of the lobby. The bartender sorted bottles behind the bar, his back to Caesar. The assassin stepped up to the counter and cleared his throat.

The bartender turned and smiled. He was thin with dark hair. His white shirt needed an iron. He said, "Good morning."

"I need to see Jakov," the killer said.

"I'm sorry. Who?"

"Jakov Perusko. Do you think I'm stupid?"

"We have two Jakovs here, my apologies. Mr. Perusko isn't here today."

"My information says otherwise."

"Your information is wrong, sir."

The bartender's hand moved beneath the counter. Caesar shot his right fist forward and hit the bartender in the mouth. The man recoiled as the impact split his lower lip. Caesar vaulted the bar, another blow sending the bartender to the floor. Caesar drew a compact pistol as two men emerged from a door at the back of the bar. Peeking over the top of the counter, he watched them scan the room. They kept their hands under their coats. Caesar rose with his pistol. He fired once. The suppressor on the snout muted the shots. The first man fell, his tan sport coat turning red as he bled through. His partner tugged free his own weapon. Caesar fired again and carved a hole through the second man's left eye. The assassin put two more rounds in the man's chest as he fell back.

Caesar vaulted the bar again, running to the corpses, dropping to a knee at the corner of the bar. He watched the door from which the gunners came. No more troops arrived. He advanced to the doorway, staying to one side. A man started yelling from the end of the narrow hallway beyond the door.

Caesar waited. He didn't want to wait too long. The last thing he needed was any guests from upstairs coming down to the lobby. The empty reception desk made him wonder if the hotel had any guests at all. Whether rooms had occupants wasn't his concern. His concern lay at the end of the hallway.

Caesar stood. He passed through the doorway, keeping

his back to the wall. He approached the half-open doorway at the end of the hall. The man on the other side of the door continued to yell for his men, and his voice took on a tinge of alarm. He knew something unpleasant was coming. Caesar had to get him before he sounded an alarm.

Caesar pushed open the door and leveled his gun on a man behind a desk.

"Jakov. Don't move."

Jakov Perusko gaped at Caesar.

"Take your hand out of the drawer and do so slowly. If I see a gun, I'll kill you."

"You have me dead to rights, whoever you are." Jakov complied. His hand came out of the drawer empty. He placed both palms on the desktop.

Caesar lowered the pistol to his hip. He took a few steps forward, enough to give him a good view of Perusko's movement, should he make any. He wasn't so close the gun runner had a chance to counter-attack.

"What did you do to my men?"

Caesar grinned.

"One's out cold on the floor, the other two are dead."

"Who are you?"

"Caesar. You know my name."

"I do. Why are you here?"

"You're quite calm for a man with a gun pointed at him."

"I've been around guns my entire life. Many have pointed guns at me in the past. Your gun doesn't scare me. Your intention with it is another matter. Why are you here?"

"Branko Zupan."

"What?"

"Are you surprised?" the killer said.

"I expected—"

"This is nothing related to your business. Tell me what I

want to know, and I'll leave. Refuse, and you'll end up like the stiffs in the bar."

Jakov Perusko cleared his throat. "What about Branko?"

"Where is he?"

"Nobody knows. He moves around a lot. New hideout every few days. His mother's ghost couldn't keep up with him."

"No, somebody knows. Maybe even you."

"I swear I do not. Branko used to work for me, yes, but he does not any longer. He hooked up with a Dutchman."

"You know how to reach him."

"He uses burner phones."

"He only calls you?"

"When he needs something."

"I don't believe you, Jakov. You need to do a better job of convincing me. People like us always know how to reach our friends."

Perusko laughed. "People like us have no friends."

"Whatever you want to call them, then. What I'm not hearing from you is an answer to my questions."

"You're going to have to kill me, Caesar. I don't have the information you want. The last time I talked to Branko was--" He stopped.

"Continue," Caesar said. Perusko's face turned white as he remained silent. He'd tipped his hand and Caesar had him by the neck.

"I don't know where Branko is right now," Perusko continued, "but there is a way to reach him. He can't know the tip came from me."

Caesar smiled. "He'll never know."

Perusko's eyes darted over Caesar's shoulder. The hinges of the door squeaked. The bloody bartender swung a bottle at Caesar's head as the killer pivoted. Caesar ducked but didn't dodge the bartender's follow-up strike. He kicked Caesar in the belly. Caesar grunted and doubled over, but he didn't let go of his gun. The assassin drove his head into the bartender's midsection. Both men collided with the wall beside the door. Caesar grunting as the bartender hammered blows into his back. Caesar returned the strikes with his left hand, slamming a fist into the bartender's gut. Both men fell on the floor, a tangle of arms and legs, and Caesar beat at him with the gun. Three solid blows to the head. The bartender's skin split and blood spilled. Caesar pushed him far enough away to get the gun between them. He fired once. The bartender flopped and lay still.

Caesar stayed on the ground, twisting to turn his gun on Perusko. The gun runner pulled a pistol from his desk drawer and leveled the gun. He smiled as he aimed but Caesar fired first. Once, twice. His pistol locked open empty, but the rounds hit where intended. Perusko's chest sprouted two holes and he dropped back into his chair. The force of his landing sent the chair smashing into the wall behind him.

Franco rose and brushed off his clothes. Slapping a fresh magazine into his gun, he approached the dead Jakov and hoped to find an item of importance. He had to hurry. He sorted through the desk clutter but found nothing related to the gun business. All the paperwork concerned the inner workings of the hotel. He patted Perusko's pockets and found a cell phone. A scan of the contact list did not reveal a number for Branko Zupan. Maybe the gun runner had been telling the truth after all. Caesar wiped the cell phone on the dead man's clothes and dropped the phone on the floor. As a lead went, Jakov Perusko was literally a dead end.

He stowed his gun under his coat but did not exit through the lobby. He found a back door to an alley and hurried to the street. He walked away from the hotel, checking his clothes as covertly as he could for bloodstains. Some blood spatter from the bartender had stained his jeans. He didn't think anybody would pay much attention.

He walked a few blocks to catch his breath. He hailed another cab to take him back to his hotel where he could ditch the clothes, clean up, and plan his next move. It was almost noon. He had all day, and the weather was wonderful.

35

WHILE CAESAR WAS GETTING READY FOR HIS NEXT MOVE, NEWS of Perusko's death spread through the underworld of Zagreb. One man particularly interested in the incident was Karlo Rozic.

Rozic held a big position in the Croatian underworld. His organization spanned the country and other parts of Eastern Europe. He sold drugs. Rozic's crew held a monopoly on distribution in the Balkan region, and he delighted in flooding Serbia with cocaine and opiates. The best way to settle the score with his old enemies was to turn them into drug addicted zombies. Bastards deserved nothing less for what they'd done to his country.

Keeping such an organization running with efficiency meant maintaining an armed force, and troops needed guns. Jakov Perusko had supplied plenty of guns during their association, but now somebody had killed Jakov.

Jakov hadn't been a friend, per se. But Rozic respected Jakov and knew the gun runner felt the same. He wanted to know who killed his countryman. He needed his crew's help to identify the enemy. Rozic wasn't sure what he'd do with the information. Strike back? Meet the new player? He'd make up his mind when he had enough data.

He'd called his men for an emergency meeting at his house, and they gathered on the balcony below his office window. They talked, drank champagne, and picked from plates of fresh fruit. He watched them stoically, like somebody tracking ants on a sidewalk. Rozic was short. During the war, he'd looked emaciated. He still maintained the look of somebody who didn't get enough to eat, but the fact was he'd always been of small stature. The command he wielded, however, was anything but slight. His orders were never questioned. He might look like a small dog, but he had the bite of a much larger one and wasn't afraid to show his power when necessary.

When he saw the last man arrive and take his seat at the outdoor table, he turned from the window and made his way downstairs.

His house sat in the green mountains north of Zagreb. He owned not only the land the house sat on, but several acres surrounding the property. He kept the area patrolled by roving team of armed guards. A wire fence marked the perimeter, with plenty of signs warning of no trespassing. He'd never had a problem with civilians straying where they shouldn't. He wasn't worried about civilians. The people with enough money to own homes in the mountains knew better than to step into somebody's business. He wasn't worried about competition, interlopers, those intent on striking at him. His men were on high alert, and they had dogs. The dogs were not only trained to sniff out intruders, but attack and bite on command. Rozic wanted prisoners if the opportunity arose.

He left the window to go and join the meeting.

Caesar blended with the environment like a chameleon. Dressed head-to-toe in green camouflage, he was one with the forest. And the forest offered plenty of concealment. He had an edge, and he couldn't say the same for the pair of Rozic goons moving ten yards from his position. They were moving toward him.

Caesar set his rifle on the ground, then slid off a submachine gun from around his back. He set the SMG next to the rifle. From the scabbard on his right hip, he withdrew a serrated knife. He moved out, cutting through the foliage on a path taking him wide of the approaching troops. One turned his direction as he drew abreast.

Caesar dived at the trooper. He tackled the gunner and fell on top of him, slashing the edge of his blade across the man's neck. The other gunner managed to cry for help as he leveled his weapon, and Caesar leaped to wrap both arms around the man's legs. The second gunner went down and was helpful enough to strike his head on a fallen tree limb. Dazed from the impact, the trooper had no defense against Caesar's next knife slash. The serrated edge opened the trooper's throat. He began choking and gagging as life went away from him.

Caesar ran back to his weapons. He slung the submachine gun across his back again, grabbed the suppressor-fitted rifle, and resumed his march. He had a near perfect view of the balcony where Rozic's men gathered. The meeting was going to prove very fortuitous.

Rozic crossed the wide balcony which stretched across the length of the rear of the house. Stilts supported the deck on the sloped ground beneath. Over the balcony wall stretched Zagreb. The city looked quiet and peaceful in the middle of the afternoon. Rozic had fought a war for his home to remain quiet and peaceful. He didn't want an intruder to mess up the status quo.

His men watched him approach. Rozic stopped at the head of the table to address them. He didn't sit down.

"We've had an incident," he began.

"With somebody who isn't part of our organization," said Blago, who argued with Rozic on any topic. Blago wanted to be in charge, but he lacked the guts and manpower to launch a coup. Even if he did take over, he knew Rozic's loyalists would shoot him. A no-win situation. So he argued a lot.

"I like that you're arguing with me, Blago, despite the champagne I've put out, and the spread of fresh fruit you're enjoying," Rozic said.

"But Jakov Perusko is no business of ours."

"We've all benefitted from Jakov's services. He's never failed to provide what we ask for, and he's never cheated us. What we need to know is if whoever killed him did so for personal reasons, or to edge into the territory and thereby threaten the rest of us. Also, I'm not sure I want to do business with somebody who killed one of our own. I'd rather remove this intruder and take over Jakov's gun business myself."

A man to Rozic's left, Drevan, said, "I've already been checking out what happened."

"What have you learned?"

"Caesar."

Rozic frowned. "What do him and Jakov have to do with each other?"

"We can ask when he gets here."

"What are you getting at?"

"You, me, everybody here, *and* Jakov, have a mutual friend in Branko Zupan."

"Oh, no."

"Caesar," Drevan said, "is looking for Zupan."

Rozic frowned. The new information was good and bad.

Blago lifted his glass of champagne. "I told you a long time ago Zupan was trouble." He put the glass to his lips and started to drink. He took a swallow, and the front of his face exploded. The glass shattered. Blood, bone, and shredded flesh joined the spread on the table.

Another quiet shot killed Drevan after he shouted, "Sniper!" and then Rozic and his remaining men dived for the hot concrete. More screams filled the air as bullets found targets. Rozic shouted for help in tipping over the table. As he grabbed the edge and helped shove, a bullet cut the air above his head. The table tipped over with a crash. Glasses crashed. The fresh fruit spread out like a big puddle. The survivors scrambled around the front side of the table for cover. They squeezed close to maximize the table's length. A bullet struck the opposite side with a *thunk*. Rozic didn't furnish the balcony with junk. The table was made of thick oak. The bullet didn't break through.

Two of Rozic's gunmen, flat on the floor inside the house, opened the patio door a crack. Rozic shouted orders. A bullet smacked the glass. The bulletproofing held. Rozic's gunners rushed away to deliver his orders to the rest of the gun crew.

From the angle of the attack, Rozic figured the sniper had placed himself on the hill left of the balcony. Maybe 50 yards away. His men, and their dogs, would find the shooter. Rozic hasn't specified dead or alive.

Never mind thinking he could talk his way through the problem. Whoever had sent Caesar to find Branko Zupan didn't care who he blasted to find what he wanted. Which meant Rozic's fight was with whoever hired Caesar, not the assassin. If his men brought in Caesar alive, he'd make the assassin talk or kill him in the process.

CAESAR CURSED as he searched for a new target. His scope put him on the balcony, but all of his targets were on the other side of the overturned table. If they made a break for the patio doors, they'd expose themselves long enough for him to fire. The Croat crime bosses were smart enough to stay put.

Then he heard the dogs.

Best laid plans and all that, Caesar thought. He wanted to soften Rozic and his men before confronting them, but he'd have to get through the troops and dogs first.

He had to abandon his position and get ready for a fight. Caesar let one last round *thump* from the muzzle of his suppressed rifle. One more shot into the table to remind Rozic somebody had him in the crosshairs. He scrambled from the rifle, snatched the compact submachine gun from his back, and turned to run up the slope behind him.

36

Four gunners, and two dogs, homed in on Caesar's position.

The four gunmen didn't care about stealth. They stomped through the foliage, shoving low branches out of the way. They snapped twigs, crushed dry leaves. The dogs breathed hard, tongues out, straining against their harnesses.

Caesar wondered if they wanted him alive.

Well, tough luck.

Caesar sat with his knees up, his submachine gun tucked into his shoulder. The dogs might have his scent but the humans didn't. He sighted along the barrel and eased back on the trigger.

"Sorry, pooch," Caesar said as the trigger snapped.

The submachine gun cracked. No suppressor this time. The first dog pitched forward and rolled. His handler tripped over the body and into Caesar's sights. The assassin worked the trigger again. The second salvo ripped through the gunner's back and left him on the ground on top of the dog.

Caesar rolled left. The remaining three gunmen opened fire, shredding the area where Caesar had been. Caesar kept rolling until he collided with a stump. He fired blind, a short burst, as he crawled behind the stump and stretched out. The second dog, released from his harness, raced toward him at a furious gallop. Saliva dripped from each corner of the animal's mouth.

Caesar fired fast. He missed. The dog leaped at him, arcing over, his mouth open to bite. Caesar rolled away from the stump, the dog chomping at him. Caesar swung at the dog, deflecting the bites, then screaming as the dog's jaw snapped closed on his left wrist. Caesar stopped, then twisted the submachine gun across his belly. He fired point blank. The force of the blast pushed the dog away as the bullets ripped open his side. Caesar shook his left arm free, but now his gun was empty. His left arm was useless and on fire with pain. And he faced the three remaining gunners.

Caesar swung the empty submachine gun at the nearest gunman, who shifted and dropped to cover. Caesar let go of the weapon and snatched his pistol from the holster on his right thigh. He fired three times, swinging the pistol left and right to cover the targets. He tried to get up, but without the support of his left hand, he couldn't rise. A gunman rose to take aim; Caesar shot him in the face.

Caesar scooted backward, dragging through the dirt and brush. He wanted to go further up the slope. Create more distance between him and the gunmen. He stopped, winded. The last two shooters spread out. They were working around obstacles to get a bead on him. Caesar winged a shot at the gunner on his left; missed. The gunner took aim. Caesar fired again. The gunner dropped with a hole in his throat spurting blood.

Caesar searched for the final gunman but couldn't see him. He wasn't going to fire blindly and hope for a hit. He needed to save ammo. He blinked to clear his sweaty eyes, wincing as he wiped with the fingers of his left hand. Blood from the dog bite had dripped between his fingertips. Movement. Leaves shuffled. Caesar fired as the last gunner emerged. The man pitched over and tumbled down the slope.

Caesar relaxed on his back, still clutching his pistol, mouth open to suck more air. His arm burned and he felt exhausted. But he still had a mission. He had to confront Rozic and ask him about Zupan. But he also needed a rest. Let Rozic and his surviving men sweat a little longer.

He lay gasping and staring at the blue sky through the gaps in the trees.

ROZIC and his men remained behind the table. The crackles of gunfire in the mountains reminded him of the war. The sweat on his brow was cold.

When the shooting faded, Rozic wiped his face and started to rise. The man on his right grabbed at his arm. He brushed off the hand.

"Did they get him?" somebody asked.

Rozic examined the worried faces of his men. His surviving crew. They'd been through a lot together but nothing like this, ever. The four followed his example and began to get up.

"I hope so," Rozic said.

He led the crew into the house. They congregated at a bar in the corner of the well-furnished room. Rozic poured four glasses of Johnny Walker. The crew drank quickly and Rozic refilled. He spilled a little on the carpet in the process but didn't care.

"What the hell is going on?" Rozic asked.

A gunshot answered him. Then another. The front door crashed open.

Rozic and his associates spread out. The man who stepped into the room from the entryway wore green camouflage. Part of his right sleeve had been torn off and wrapped around his left wrist. Blood seeped through the wrap. The man covered the four with his pistol.

"Nobody move."

Rozic said, "You're the boss."

But one of Rozic's men started forward. Caesar shot him in the stomach. The man slapped his hands to his gun, let out a howl and collapsed. Two others moved to help but Caesar warned them to stay put.

"If you want to live, answer my questions."

Rozic drank from his glass. His hand shook. He thought of putting the glass down on the bar but decided not to. He forced a weak smile at the intruder.

"Want a drink?"

"No."

"You gave us quite a reminder of the war with the show in the forest."

Caesar only smiled. But the corners of his mouth dropped as pain flashed across his face.

"You must be Caesar," Rozic continued. He ignored the low wail of his wounded man. "I wish we were meeting under better circumstances."

Caesar inhaled sharply and leaned against the wall. But his gun didn't waver.

"Start asking," Rozic said, "so we can help our man."

"Branko Zupan," Caesar said. "Where is he?"

"He recruited two of my men. Milos and Klaus. They're pretty tough. They were looking for property in Wales, I heard. Might be his safe house."

"Uh-huh."

"I hired Zupan once. One of my guys you killed on the balcony thought it was a bad idea."

Caesar took another labored breath. "You should have listened."

"One of the dogs get you?"

"Yeah."

"Hurts like hell, I bet."

"Your dogs are dead."

"I figured. Anyway, Wales. I don't know exactly where, but it shouldn't be too hard to find them."

"Okay."

"You going to shoot any more of us?"

"No."

"Okay," Rozic said.

Caesar pushed away from the wall.

"Want to help us clean up at least?"

Caesar walked backwards as he exited. His gun never left the three standing men.

Rozic sighed with relief when Caesar finally departed. He poured another drink as two of his men tended to the wounded man on the floor.

37

FIRST, HE NEEDED A DOCTOR.

Caesar cleaned and dressed the dog bite in his hotel room, but he wanted a real doctor to look at the wound too. His associates in Paris identified an off-the-books doctor in the city, but the man wasn't cheap. Caesar didn't care. The doctor took a look at the bite and torn skin and gave him more bandages. He also provided a disinfectant fluid to wash the wound each time he changed bandages. Caesar paid the man and retreated to his hotel room to rest and recover for 24 hours.

He didn't stay idle. Via secure phone calls and VPN internet connections, he put out the word about Wales. Caesar's people had no informants in Wales who could poke around. Caesar ordered his associate Alexia to fly to Wales and look around herself. After what he'd faced with Rozic, he figured another pair of hands might be a good idea.

Since Alexia was on the job, Caesar decided to stay put another day before departing Zagreb.

Raven finally felt human again.

He still had to take it easy. The soreness and aches hadn't gone away one hundred percent, but at least he was out of bed. Stepping under the first hot shower he'd had in days, he decided not to worry if he used all the hot water. He began washing away everything but the mental pain left behind with Megan's death.

While under the hot spray, he turned the sadness to thoughts of revenge. He'd seen the face of the man who sent the killers. All he required was his name. And Raven had a hunch his name was Branko Zupan. The man who had sent Shaw, Webb, and Buchanan after him and Megan in Barcelona at the start.

Raven washed his hair. He avoided the area of stitches on the side of his head. Ana Gray's doctor had shaved the area before applying the stitches. He decided he might as well shave the rest.

He turned off the water and stepped out to dry with a big towel. Ana didn't skimp. The towel was thick and soft. The bathroom floor had real tile. The counter was marble, now with a sheen of moisture from the steam of the shower. Stainless steel fixtures for the sink. Nothing cheap.

He summed up his action plan as he dried.

Branko Zupan. How to find him?

Perhaps through the Dutch Syndicate connection he was once affiliated with.

Oscar Morey was still working the Dutch angle and Raven expected an update soon. Morey had feared the worst when Raven dropped off the radar. Their conversation 24 hours earlier assured Raven's friend and mentor the only thing Raven needed was some rest.

Raven wrapped the towel around his waist and left the bathroom. Ana had provided a full wardrobe. Raven dressed in comfortable slacks and a polo shirt and slipped his feet into a pair of sandals.

He found Ana on the balcony looking toward Barcelona airport. A passenger jet flew over the house. She sat at a table with a bowl of fruit on either side. Raven took the empty chair. When the jet noise faded, she spoke.

"Breakfast will be another ten minutes."

Raven grabbed a fork and began eating slices of cantaloupe, honeydew, and pineapple.

"I could eat a horse," he told her.

She laughed. "Try a stack of bacon, eggs, and pancakes."

Raven frowned. A piece of her usual outfit was missing. "Where's the diamond necklace?"

She smiled. "After breakfast."

Raven savored a slice of pineapple. The natural sweetness was amazing.

"After we eat, we can go over some stuff," she said. "Your friend Oscar and I have been coordinating. Our intel matches."

Raven nodded. Oscar had told him as much. The pair had connected while Raven recovered in bed. "Good." He drank from a glass of orange juice.

Her promise of a big breakfast delivered. She ate a little while Raven ate until he thought he'd explode. He ate like he hadn't had any food in days. In reality, he hadn't had anything more than an IV drip while lying unconscious in the spare bedroom.

"How are you holding up?" she said.

"I'll manage."

It was the only answer he gave. She didn't ask any further questions about his state of mind.

"You can forget the pictures," he told her. "To make sure we're clear. When I find them—"

"You'll destroy them."

"I will."

"Oh, well. It was worth a try."

He didn't see another option. He had to remove the threat to the United States. He had to put a stop to the pain the pictures had caused.

RAVEN SAT to Ana's left as she opened a folder, clicked on files, and filled the widescreen with pictures. The photos, some older than others, featured various locations around the world. But Raven spotted the common link between the pictures right away. Each picture showed the same man. Branko Zupan. *The Face*. Confirmed.

"I found as many as I could," Ana said, "and there are more if—"

"It's him. Who are the two women?"

"The Lovrekovic sisters, Jasna and Petra. Jasna is the tall one and a few years older than Petra. They were kids during the war between Croatia and Serbia. Families dead. It's how they got their start. Instead of resettling after the war, they fell in with various bad actors. Made their money with criminal activities."

"Uh-huh."

"You're not the only one looking for him," she said. "There are a lot of rumors coming out of Zagreb, where Zupan and the women are from. Somebody's shooting their way through his former associates to find him."

Raven ignored the detail. He wasn't surprised. He frowned as the significance dawned on him. Who else could know Zupan now possessed the blackmail pictures?

"Who is after him and why?" he asked.

"I don't have a crystal ball. I only have people sniffing around and it might take time to answer."

"Forget it. What about Oscar's check on the Dutch angle?"

Ana cleared the screen and opened two new pictures. A man and a woman.

"Derick Vokkert and his main squeeze, Evelien Eulen. Part of the Amsterdam crime fraternity known as *penose*. Know what that means?"

"Separate organized gangs instead of concentrated families like the Italians use. More like the Irish gangs than anything. What's he into?"

"Drugs, prostitution, the usual. Mostly drugs. Zupan worked for him after leaving Zagreb. Whoever is shooting up Zagreb might be looking in the wrong place."

"Or," Raven said, "Vokkert sent somebody to find him, and the starting point is Zagreb."

"Why do you think so?"

"Zupan's off the reservation and Vokkert isn't happy."

"He's a dead end to you then. You want to track the person looking for Zupan. Let him do all the hard work."

"No, Vokkert will have something for me. He's sent somebody after Zupan because he can't reach him, but there's a way. He'll tell me or I'll take what I want off his corpse."

"We're only guessing," Ana said. "Vokkert might be directing Zupan's efforts."

"All I know is I'm done talking."

"Are you leaving right away?"

"I have to."

38

CAESAR MET HIS OPERATIVE, ALEXIA, IN WALES AFTER recuperating in Zagreb for three days. Alexia had been busy during her scouting mission. She visited several realtors, telling them about a fictitious search for a new home. During the conversations, she asked about recent sales. Every realtor she spoke to was eager to brag about their big wins. She tried to lead them into talking about homes of a particular type. Homes away from the population, but still close enough for basic needs and easy road access. It was Alexia's idea Zupan would pick an isolated spot. Caesar would have preferred cover inside a city's limit. But from what the boss had related to her, she figured she was correct. Worse case, they started a new search within the villages and towns close to the coast.

Alexia made a list of the homes and plotted their locations on her computer map.

When Caesar saw the list, the pictures, and Alexia's notes, he told her to get ready to check each location. Covertly, of course. They couldn't go knocking on doors pretending they were selling vacuum cleaners. Such improvisations had worked in the past. Came in quite handy, actually. But Branko Zupan was not any other target. Caesar had to approach him carefully. There was no room for error.

Caesar and Alexia found Zupan and his crew in the third house on the list.

Caesar lay prone on a small rise fifty yards from the house. Through the scope of his sniper rifle, he watched Milos and Klaus, the two gunners, make a security check around the house. They made their circle, stood around a bit, and went back inside.

He and Alexia each wore a wireless com unit. Alexia was somewhere on the opposite side of the house. He said, "Got the two shooters. See anything on your side?"

Caesar waited. Alexia didn't reply.

"Lexi, do you read?"

A voice not Alexia's responded. "Hello, Caesar."

A woman.

"Who is this?" he said.

"Look behind you."

Caesar, still prone, turned as instructed. Fifteen yards away, crouched behind a boulder, was another woman. She wasn't speaking. But she held an automatic rifle on him.

"Do you see?" the woman in his ear said.

"I see."

"If you have a pistol, take it out and toss it."

Caesar removed the handgun from under his coat and threw it away. The gun landed somewhere with a thud.

"Put up your hands."

"Where's my partner?"

"Never mind, Caesar. Hands up."

Caesar clenched his teeth. He lifted his hands as he rolled over and sat up. The woman at the boulder stood and gestured for him to come forward.

The two women, Jasna and Petra, escorted Caesar into the house. Alexia was there on her knees, on the floor, with one of the Rozic gunmen standing over her. The second gunner grabbed Caesar by the neck and shoved him to his knees next to Alexia. Caesar looked at his associate, who stared at the floor, and didn't acknowledge her boss.

The two women with their automatic rifles stayed behind them. The two gunmen remained in front. And then they stepped aside to let Branko Zupan stand between them.

"Derick must have written you one hell of a check," Zupan said.

"It was enough," Caesar said. He had to look up to meet Zupan's eyes and doing so strained his neck. He felt the ache right away.

"Your mistake was murdering my old friends. I heard about it."

"Uh-huh."

"Killing me won't stop anything."

"It'll stop you from being a threat to your boss."

"Derick is paranoid. I'm not interested in sabotaging his work."

Caesar said nothing.

"You could do better than shooting me, Caesar."

"Really."

Zupan dropped into a squat. He was finally at Caesar's eye level, and the assassin's neck appreciated the reprieve.

"Want to know what I can do for you, Caesar?"

"Sure."

"I can change your life."

Caesar scoffed. "How?"

Zupan smiled. He stood and crossed the room to a table, where he retrieved an envelope. He knelt in front of Caesar again and opened the envelope.

"This is what it's all about. Look at these pictures."

Zupan took his time flipping through the photographs. He held them so Caesar had a good look. Alexia leaned over to look too. Caesar's expression started as surprise, turned to a frown, and ended with a laugh.

"I've heard the rumors—"

"Now you know the truth. This is the prize, Caesar." Zupan returned the photos to the envelope. He tossed it onto a nearby chair.

"When the US finds out I have them," Zupan said, "they'll never bother me again. The chase stops, Caesar. I'll be free. My girls will be free. You can benefit from this, or I can put you in a hole."

"What do you mean?"

"Throw in with me. Like Milos and Klaus here. They knew staying with Rozic was a dead end."

Caesar's expression softened. He liked the idea but saw the flaw. Presidents in the US had short tenures. The threat of the pictures becoming public wouldn't hold forever. But then he reconsidered. Even with the current president out of office, the snapshots could cause a scandal. They'd ruin his post-presidential "elder statesman" role.

Zupan might have landed on what Caesar had been looking for a long time. The ticket out of the killing business. He could even wait long enough to take them from Zupan and his women and enjoy the fruit alone.

"What do you say, Caesar? It's right now or you're in a ditch. I'll throw your lady friend on top of you."

"If I saw yes, she goes free."

Zupan pressed his lips together in thought.

"All right. I'll let her go."

Zupan stood. Caesar straightened his clothes. Alexia stood. Caesar offered her an encouraging nod. Then a gun exploded. Caesar jumped back as a bullet split Alexia's face. Blood splattered on Caesar's clothes.

He pivoted to Zupan, who held the smoking pistol. He swung it to Caesar.

"Do you ever think I'd let you in?"

Zupan fired again.

39

RAVEN DEPARTED BARCELONA FOR AMSTERDAM WITHOUT weapons. Ana promised to arrange with contacts in the area to provide what he needed or wanted. He'd need a replacement for his lost Nighthawk .45. Ana's crew in Wexford had not been able to liberate from police custody. He felt declawed without his Talon, but in the end a gun is a gun. He'd make do with what Ana's contact had available.

His new fake Canadian passport identified him as James Blanski. His visa, Ana promised, was one of the best forgeries she'd ever seen. He landed in Amsterdam, cleared customs, and collected his single suitcase. He felt funny traveling as a civilian. No special X-ray proof bottom to the piece of luggage Ana had given him. No hidden compartments in his carry-on. He had nothing but the basics. Clothes, accessories, a laptop computer, and a pair of paperback westerns. This was the first time in a long time where he was out of his natural element. His condition would change soon. Within a few hours he'd feel the comfortable weight of a weapon once again.

He found a taxi to take him to his hotel. The city

reminded him of his home in Stockholm. Canals cut through the city, creating narrow streets quickly clogged with traffic. On the surface, he could migrate to Amsterdam, but he saw a deal killer right away. There were plenty of house boats lining the wider canals. But there was also too much canal traffic for his taste. One side of every house boat faced a busy sidewalk. Amsterdam was too crowded for the isolation and privacy Raven preferred.

Homes and apartments also caught his attention. The narrow domiciles were pressed together in a Cuban sandwich-style of construction. A lot of color—no grays, no drab steel-and-glass, thank you. At a stop light, he watched a pair of men wrap thick ropes around a large chair. They then pulled on an opposite rope wound through a pulley at the top of the building. The chair left the ground on its way up. Somebody half out of a window midway pulled the chair through the open window. Space inside was too narrow. Nobody brought furniture upstairs by hand. None of it would fit. The city engineers devised the pulley system to help people get furniture into homes. Every building in the city was so equipped.

The light changed and the taxi drove on. Presently the driver dropped Raven at his hotel. He carried his luggage into the lobby to check in.

In his room, Raven set the suitcase on the bed, and laughed as he looked around. The room was small and cramped. He might have had more space in a coffin.

He checked his watch and glanced out the window. The digital clock on the nightstand gave off a small buzz. He'd have preferred a ticking clock, and another tangible sound to fill the silence. He wanted noise to drown out his thoughts.

He went to the window. The street below was busy with a mix of bicycles and cars. More bicycles than cars. They had a dedicated lane. Bicycles were big in Amsterdam. In the city center, bicycles and public transport was the only means of getting around. No cars allowed. Tough for quick getaways. Raven planned to hit Derick Vokkert hard, and he'd have to modify his approach. Avoid the city center, he decided. And if he wasn't careful, he risked drawing civilians into a cross-fire. Rule Two. He'd flirted with breaking Rule One and now he was paying the price. He wasn't going to break Rule Two.

What might have he done differently? Or had his ghosts orchestrated events the same way he'd justified Megan and Sebastian? Or was it bad luck? He felt a wave of grief wash over him but turned it to anger. Vokkert would know some-thing. If he'd hired another player to find Zupan, he'd have a progress report. A lead would shake loose once he'd rattled their cage enough.

He checked his watch again. Still a few hours before he met Ana's gun dealer. Instead of laying down for a nap, he went downstairs to the lobby restaurant. He had to keep the basic functions in mind if he was going to be in any shape to do what he needed. Avenge Megan. Nothing else mattered.

IN AMSTERDAM, A "COFFEE SHOP" didn't serve coffee exclusively. You visited a coffee shop to buy marijuana. Raven found the place he needed in the Red Light District. The tourist crowd didn't notice him. The undercover police officers watching the crowd saw through him. They recog-nized an aura around him. They knew he was going to be trouble. He'd need another way out when his business finished.

He stepped inside and wished for a nose plug. Goddamn weed. He could shit on the floor and create a better smell. But at least Amsterdam forced idiot potheads into designated spaces. It kept the stink off the street.

He crossed the narrow space, lined with full tables and chairs. Smoke drifted below the ceiling. He reached the counter. The woman behind the register said hello.

"I'm here to see a man named Damien."

The woman said hang on and disappeared through an open doorway behind her. She returned with a man who said, "What's your name?"

"Jim. Ana sent me. Said to tell you to bring out the iron."

"Come on back."

Raven followed the man through the doorway. He might not have come to the coffee shop armed, but he was still ready for a fight. He could use his hands and feet as well as a pistol.

The office and hallways in back were well-lighted with no areas where somebody might hide. Ana was providing the weapons free of charge; it wasn't as if Raven was carrying money to steal.

Damien went to a safe in the wall behind his desk. Quick spin of the dial and he wrenched the safe open. He pulled two metal cases from the safe and set them on his desk. One case was larger than the other.

"I have a handgun and a submachine gun for you. Ammo, mags, suppressors. You'll get night-vision, grenades, few other things too."

Raven stepped closer to see the hardware. The small case contained a pistol he had not yet had the pleasure of handling. Damien lifted the blue-steel SIG-Sauer P-210 from the case and handed it to Raven. The nine-millimeter autoloader had checked wood grips and felt good in his hand. The gun had many of the same controls as the Nighthawk Custom. The thumb safety, slide stop, magazine release, and grip angle mirrored the M1911-style piece he'd carried for so many years. He snapped back the slide to confirm the gun was empty, let it slam forward, and aimed at the wall. He squeezed the trigger. The hammer snapped home with a solid click. He'd have to practice a little, but the gun would conform to his hand.

"What else?"

The larger case contained a compact submachine gun. He checked the chamber. The Heckler & Koch MP5K felt light but solid. Raven dry fired. The snap of the internal hammer sounded good. Closer inspection showed a thin coat of oil on the moving parts.

"Okay," Raven said.

"I have the other stuff down the hall. Holster for the pistol and sling for the HK too. Excuse me."

"Is there a stock for the HK?" Raven asked as Damien departed.

"No."

"Hey."

Damien turned.

"Sniper rifle?"

The other man nodded. "Hang on."

Raven checked the MP5K again. Shooting without a stock might be tough, but he couldn't think of a better weapon with which to lay down a pattern of fire. Beggars and choosers and all that.

Damien returned with the promised extras, a duffel bag, and a long hardcase. Raven checked the powerful rifle inside and approved. He loaded everything but the long case into the bag.

"Is there another way out of here?" he asked.

"Want to avoid the cops?"

"You read my mind."

Damien gave him directions for another route out of the area. Raven wanted to avoid the eyes of the undercover cops. They might want to know what he was carrying.

40

AXEL BORG HAD LESS THAN THIRTY MINUTES TO LIVE AND didn't know it.

He browsed the warehouse floor with an M95 mask over his face. The crew working the two rows of tables wore similar masks. They had to. The crew was filling baggies with cocaine, and nobody desired unwanted contact with the narcotic. The product would be on the street within 48 hours; and on a ship to other points on the globe within 72.

Borg's warehouse, disguised from without as a metal fabrication plant, was off the Noordzeekanal, near the S150 motorway. On the opposite bank, a much busier warehouse / industrial area lay. Borg's side wasn't as packed; plenty of open space surrounded the warehouse. The space allowed hi-def security cameras on the roof to catch stray movement.

Axel Borg occupied a low rung in Vokkert's *penose* but he turned the biggest profit. He was tall and blonde-haired but looked unassuming. The quintessential Dutchman. He blended in and raised no alarms with his lifestyle. Borg believed in saving his pennies for the future.

But his time was running out.

Borg checked on the gunmen covering the warehouse interior. Each shooter toted a SIG MPX Copperhead and looked ready to put the submachine guns to use. Four men inside; two patrolled outside.

Borg climbed a set of steps to the upper level. He returned to his office. He had several logistical puzzles to work out. Getting the product shipped was the most stressful of his tasks. Luckily the smugglers they contracted with never tried pulling a fast one. The consequences weren't worth a quick buck.

RAVEN WAITED outside the perimeter fence.

Through night-vision goggles, he scanned the open yard around the drug warehouse. Vokkert's people kept the overgrowth down. Hard-packed dirt, with nothing to provide cover, lay between him and the building. He'd circled the property once already had found no alternative entry points. He had to cross the no man's land and get inside the building.

He wore the SIG P-210 in a shoulder harness and the MP5K submachine gun across his back. He'd hooked several frag and phosphorous grenades on his chest rig. He planned to burn the place to the ground. Whether he killed everyone inside didn't matter. But anybody who crossed his gun sights was fair game.

Finally, he detected movement through the NVGs. Two armed men near the building. They had an irregular patrol pattern and spent most of their time on the canal side of the warehouse.

He watched without moving for five minutes. The two guards moved on, turning the corner to the canal side once again.

Raven used a pair of wire cutters to snip the chain link. He had to work fast. The drug warehouse may have been isolated, but a firefight wasn't an event the neighbors could ignore. One last snip and he stowed the cutters. Raven moved through the gap and advanced twenty yards before dropping flat. He waited two minutes, then rose and raced forward again. Another drop and pause. Around the left corner of the warehouse, the patrolling gunmen appeared once again. Raven froze.

The guards spread out in a combat crouch and took cover. The voice of one carried to Raven's ears. The man was talking into a radio.

They'd spotted him.

AXEL BORG TOOK the radio call at the same time he saw the intruder on his office monitors.

The movement on the dark screen was subtle, and he wasn't 100% certain until the intruder moved again. The guard had been right. He alerted the four in-door gunners. He didn't want to disturb the workers so he told the gun crew to get in defense positions quietly.

Borg set aside his paperwork and reached for a panel. He flicked two switches. Bright lights outside filled the rear field with illumination. He used another switch to zoom one of the cameras at the intruder. The infiltrator was centered in the middle monitor.

Borg watched the man snatch a pistol from under his right arm and open fire. The muzzle of his gun flashed twice.

THE LIGHTS SNAPPED ON. Raven shut his eyes and swept the NVGs off his face. Grabbing for the SIG pistol, he thrust the gun forward. The two gunners rose and leveled their guns. Raven fired twice. The nine-millimeter cracked and the rounds found a home. One of the spotlights blinked out.

Raven moved left. The light he shot out returned a portion of the area to semi-darkness. He ran into the black. The two gunners opened fire with rapid single shots. The parabellum manglers from the snouts of their weapons split the air above Raven. He went into a tuck and roll and stretched out again. He extended the P-210 and the pistol cracked again and again. One of the gunners dropped. The other ran back to the building. Raven fired at him but missed.

The gunner yelled into his radio again. Raven hurried to fill the SIG with a fresh mag. He stowed the pistol in the shoulder harness and unslung the MP5K. Flicking the selector from Safe to 3-Round Burst, he charged forward.

The edge of the dirt field ended at blacktop. The warehouse crew stacked their junk on the pavement. Raven found enough to hide. Stacks of pallets, a line of trucks, empty oil barrels.

Raven ducked behind pallets and listened. More voices. Nobody spoke over a radio, but outside, in person. More gunners. One of them took charge. He began issuing orders. Raven grabbed a phosphorous grenade from his chest rig and hurried to the row of pick-up trucks.

A burst from the MP5K blasted holes in the gas tank of one truck. Fuel spilled and formed a large puddle. Raven pulled the pin on the grenade and dropped it into the puddle. The grenade rolled through the liquid and by the time it sparked, Raven was back behind the pallets. The grenade popped, spewing smoke and sparks, and the puddle of fuel ignited. The flames flashed under the first and second trucks. And then the explosions happened.

The first truck went up in a thundering fireball; the second followed. The shock wave rocked the pallets. Two from the top fell and landed on their edges. They fell inches from Raven and he scooted away fast. The pallets toppled over with a smack. He turned to peek through a gap. Fire ate at the next two trucks. His eyes stung from the thick smoke. He put the NVGs over his eyes and left the pallets.

The gunners closed in. Raven brought up the MP5K and started firing. Two gunners fell, and the rest broke formation. Two attempted to circle the yard to flank Raven. He moved through the pallets. The thick smoke grew heavier, mixing with the acrid scent of melting rubber.

Raven pitched a frag grenade behind him. Pivoting, he pulled the trigger fast, then rolled towards oil barrels. The frag grenade detonated with a thump accompanied by screams. Scratch the flankers. Bullets smacked through the oil drums. Raven flattened as much as he could. He fired around the barrels and hit a gunner in the foot. The shooter yelled and stumbled; a follow-up burst silenced the gunner for good.

Raven pitched another frag grenade up and over the barrels. He was aiming for the wall of the warehouse. Movement on his right. The last gunner fired through gaps in the pallets, his rounds splitting wood on their way to Raven. But the wood deflected the rounds. They passed uncomfortably close as Raven twisted and fell against the barrels. They fell over with a crash, blocking Raven's view. As he hit the ground, the MP5K flew from his grasp.

The last gunner stepped around the pallets. Raven snatched out his pistol and shot him in the head. He put away the SIG and grabbed the submachine gun. His frag grenade had ripped a hole in the warehouse wall. Stray shots came at him from inside. Raven stayed low and tossed a second and third phosphorous grenade through the hole. He followed with another frag. He ran around to the canal side while shoving a full mag into the MP5K.

41

Axel Borg stayed put in his office long enough to alert Vokkert to the raid. He then ran like a frightened fox with a chicken in his mouth when the trucks exploded. Borg told the crew to get out. They didn't need a second suggestion. Borg took out a pistol to cover their exit. He was alone in the warehouse when a grenade blast ripped a hole in the wall.

Two options competed for Borg's decision. He could run for his life or go down with the ship. Shaking with nervous tension, covered in cold sweat, he hesitated. Borg didn't want to deal with Vokkert's wrath if he ran. The boss would not be happy if he cut and run.

The intruder approached the hole. Borg fired. Grenades flew through the gap. Nuts! Borg turned and ran for the exit. If his gunmen had failed, how much of a chance did he have?

He crashed through the exit door. The night was cool but smoke filled the air and made him choke.

Raven stopped and braced to fire as a lone man ran out. He squeezed the trigger. The figure cried out as the nine-millimeter hollow-points ripped through his back. The man fell face first, but still moved. He was trying to get up despite the holes in him. *Game guy*, Raven thought.

Raven walked over and fired another tri-burst into the back of Borg's head.

He turned to look into the warehouse. Flames inside. The phosphorous was burning with intensity, igniting everything flammable in its path. With all the processing chemicals inside, the blaze would grow intense. Vokkert's end-of-the-quarter balance sheet was about to be a little short.

It was time to go. Raven put the inferno behind him and escaped the way he'd arrived.

He was only getting started.

And the night was still young.

He had two more names on the hit list, and Raven wasn't going to stop until he'd finished.

———————————

ELO MOGENSEN RANKED HIGHER than Axel Borg. Mogensen was in Vokkert's inner circle. Losing a key member of his team would be a hard pill to swallow.

Raven obeyed the speed limit as he drove his rental through the night. He followed the S150 to the S118 connector and picked up the A10 back to the heart of the city. He continued south. Raven's eyes still stung from the truck fires and his clothes reeked. The dried sweat on his skin made him feel sticky and uncomfortable.

Raven drove an hour south, keeping an eye on the gas gauge. He could still make it back to his hotel. Stopping for fuel dressed as he was and loaded with guns wasn't an appealing option. Mack Bolan never had to stop for gas; some guys had all the luck, he mused.

To escape the cramped confines of Amsterdam, Elo

Mogensen lived south of the city. A stone wall surrounded his large home. A center gate led to a long driveway ending at the front door. Raven had no intention of going over the wall. He'd had enough close combat for the night; plus, he had no idea how many gunners waited for him. There were other avenues to hitting a target.

He parked off the road at the base of a hill one mile from the house. From the trunk, Raven took out a long hardcase. The last gift from Ana. He hiked up the hill into the trees.

He had to navigate via his night vision goggles, and it cost twenty minutes. But he found a proper hiding spot. His position overlooked the rear balcony connected with Mogensen's lavish bedroom.

Oscar and Ana's intel on Vokkert and his organization had so far been spot-on. He hoped the trend continued. He slowly flipped the catches on the hardcase and lifted the lid. He eased the Steyr SSG-69 from the case. He eased into shooting position and tucked the stock into his shoulder. Through the scope, the balcony doors and bedroom appeared in sharp focus.

If Mogensen maintained a heavy gun crew on the outer grounds, Raven didn't notice. If they patrolled the region surrounding the house, he'd deal with them later. What he wanted right now was Mogensen in the crosshairs. And all he had to do was wait. Within fifteen minutes, the quarry stepped into the kill zone.

A growing shadow on the bedroom floor tipped off Mogensen's presence. The man was talking rapidly into a cell phone. The alarm had been sounded; the crew knew they were under attack. He closed one French door and was reaching for the other when Raven touched the trigger. The crack split the air and hammered Raven's ears. But he rode the recoil and re-centered the scope. Mogensen pitched backward with the top of his head gone. Raven didn't stick around. He packed up and retraced his steps back to the car.

One more off the list.

RAVEN DROVE BACK TO AMSTERDAM. He'd stowed the weapons in the trunk and traded his black pullover for a plain T-shirt and light jacket. He looked almost normal. He'd pass public muster for a short time. At the late hour, pushing four a.m., there'd only be a few stragglers in the hotel lobby. Nobody would notice him.

He dialed a number on the burner phone Ana had supplied him.

Kasper Dam was another member of the Vokkert brain trust, and Raven had selected him to deliver a message.

"Yes?"

"You sound nervous, Kasper."

"Who is this?"

"Mogensen is dead and you're next unless you do exactly as I say."

"Who *are* you?"

"I'm the man who blew up your drug warehouse and killed Mogensen."

"You haven't answered my question, Mr. Marksman."

"Tell Vokkert I want Zupan. I want Zupan delivered to me alive."

"Why?"

"So I can cut his throat."

"And you'll keep hitting us until we do what you want."

"You're smarter than you look, Kasper. I see why Vokkert puts so much faith in you."

"And if I tell you instead we're going to cut off your fingers and feed them to you?"

Raven laughed. "You have to catch me first."

He ended the call and dropped the phone on the passenger seat. Burner phones were not a good idea long-term; they could be tracked as easily as a regular phone. He wouldn't need the phone much longer.

It'll be over soon, Megan.

He drove on.

42

DERICK VOKKERT HANDED THE GLASS OF RED WINE TO Evelien. She sat on a leather couch in his big living room. The drapes throughout the house, including the living room, were closed. After the sniper killed Mogensen, Vokkert wasn't going to take chances. The house was off Amsteldijk Zuid with a canal view, and normally Vokkert considered it a safe haven. Now, it felt like a prison. A madman out there wanted to kill him. He'd started by killing one key man and several others, as well as destroying a major profit center. Vokkert didn't want to set one foot outside. He didn't know what awaited him beyond the safety of the house.

And Evelien, annoyingly, took the news with a smirk on her face.

"This isn't funny," he told her. Vokkert didn't sit. He paced, holding his own glass of wine in his left hand.

"It's exciting," she said. He walked behind the couch. She didn't turn her head to track him. "We haven't had this much action—"

"Stop."

She shrugged and swallowed a mouthful of wine.

"Somebody *murdered* men I grew up with in cold blood," he said. "I don't think it's funny or exciting."

"What are we going to do?"

He'd told his surviving crew to scatter during several frantic phone calls during the past few hours. He'd been up all night. The sun was rising. But he couldn't see the dawn with the drapes closed.

"I wanted to prevent this," Vokkert said, continuing to circle the room.

"Too late."

He glared at her but she wasn't looking his way. She also wasn't wrong, but he didn't like her attitude.

"Either we have to fight or find a way to turn over Zupan."

"We don't have Zupan," Evelien said. "And Caesar—"

"Is probably dead."

No update from Caesar after he left Zagreb spoke volumes. The silence meant Zupan had emerged from their encounter victorious.

"Call Zupan," Evelien suggested.

"If calling Zupan solved anything, I wouldn't have sent Caesar."

"Try him again. Tell him to come and take responsibility."

Vokkert scoffed. "Might be worth a shot." He finally paused to drink some wine.

Evelien made no further comment. But he knew what she was thinking. And he had no other choice but to put her to work.

"I'll try reaching Zupan."

"What about me?"

"You've been waiting to ask me, haven't you?"

She smiled.

"We'll set something up with this killer. Do your worst. Mogensen, Borg and the others deserve justice."

"I'll call the girls."

"Uh-huh."

She set her glass on the wooden coffee table and left the couch. She sauntered to Vokkert and kissed him. The gang boss was more annoyed than aroused and didn't respond. She stepped back.

"I thought you'd never ask!"

"You're crazy."

Evelien laughed and returned to her wine.

RAVEN SLEPT late and rose around one in the afternoon. After a shower and shave he ordered lunch. He ate without distraction from the television.

When he finished, he set the dishes in the hallway and returned to the table. He wanted to sort through his notes, all the information provided by Oscar and Ana Gray.

How much was she worth?

Raven pushed the thought away and tried to concentrate.

He couldn't spend too much time shaking cages. The risk was too high. He needed to strike directly at Vokkert if the gang boss refused Raven's terms. He knew, by now, Vokkert was well aware of those terms as he calculated the damage caused overnight.

Can't you let it go?

Raven pushed his notes away in disgust. He turned on the TV and didn't bother adjusting the station. He used the remote to raise the volume.

But the noise did no good.

You're going to ruin everything.

Was it him thinking or the ghosts talking?

Zupan had taken somebody from him and Raven wanted to take something back. He had not been in love with Megan.

How could he with such a short time between them? What she'd given him was *hope*. Hope that his lone wolf battle might not be as lonely any longer. Hope there might be a new ally in his struggle who had her own reasons for fighting too.

Zupan couldn't return the optimism to Raven's life, but Raven could *remove* Zupan from existence. He had to accept his war without end might continue, and end, with him standing alone. There was no room for anybody else.

Raven felt for the locket he'd almost lost in Wexford had Ana not intervened. Maybe a lone play was for the best. He'd made a vow in silence and alone at the start of his war; he might as well carry on the same. Despite the toll taken. Somewhere an award waited for him.

She was worth a lot to me.

He turned off the television and returned to his work.

RAVEN HIT the road around evening. He wanted to see Vokkert's place close up and see whether a strike was viable or not. Scare the boss to his bones, and he might come across with what Raven wanted. He'd told Vokkert he wanted Zupan delivered to him. No way Vokkert would hand him over without a fight. No way would Vokkert let Raven's attacks go unanswered. Before he made any attempt to comply, he'd want to fry Raven's head in oil. Raven had to make sure he kept up the pressure.

He found the cluster of homes off Amsteldijk Zuid south of the city. No parking on the canal side of the street. He drove until he found the Amstel Horse Hotel, currently closed, and parked the car. He exited to the occasional sound and constant smell of horses boarded in the stables.

He retraced his route to Vokkert's on foot. The canal view

was nice, a few boats passing along the curvy waterway, more homes on the opposite side. The homes opposite were more spaced out and isolated, unlike Vokkert's place. On Vokkert's side, the homes faced the canal with a wide patch of green grass behind them. The field was plush and green and fed by the Ringsloot waterway behind them. If Vokkert had chosen to use the closeness of his neighbors as a shield, he'd chosen well. Raven vetoed any idea of hitting the house. A fight would violate Rule Two.

The night wind blew cold. Raven shivered despite his jacket. He returned to the horse hotel, his nose twitching at the odor, and climbed back into his rental. He drove away heading north.

The burner phone in his short pocket rang. He answered. "What is it?"

The caller's voice surprised him.

43

"This is Derick Vokkert."

"Derick! Buddy! I just left your place, dude. Nice view you have."

"Yes, it is."

Raven laughed. "Do you have somebody for me or do we get to test how good your window glass is?"

"We will pay you in full," Vokkert said.

"I'll be disappointed if this isn't a trap."

"I told you. *Paid in full.* Who are you, anyway?"

"This is Sam Raven. You know my name."

Vokkert let silence grow between them.

"Are you reconsidering your plans, Mr. Vokkert?"

"We will see you late tonight." Vokkert gave the location and a time. Raven didn't need to write down either detail. He had no plans to be at the meet.

When Vokkert stopped talking, Raven said, "I'll be there. Don't disappoint me, Mr. Vokkert."

"See you soon, Mr. Raven."

"One more thing."

"Yes?"

"Make sure your kill crazy girlfriend shows up, okay?"

"You've made your last joke, Mr. Raven."

"You sure?"

The call ended.

VOKKERT POCKETED HIS PHONE. He watched Evelien at the glass dining table. She sat with both hands working a laptop keyboard, her eyes on the screen. She typed a series of commands.

"He was here," Vokkert said.

She didn't turn away from the computer. "If the drapes were open you might have noticed."

He grunted and wandered over to her. He leaned his right hand on the back of her chair. She stopped typing.

"Is he on the security footage?"

"Here he is when Axel turned on the lights." She tilted the monitor up so he could see.

Raven's picture was centered on the computer screen. Vokkert felt glad for the decision to store security footage on the Cloud. A server at the warehouse would have burned with the rest of the building.

Vokkert stared at Raven's face. The guns, grenades, the focused expression. Yeah, he knew Sam Raven by reputation. Vokkert didn't feel a chill, or anger. He felt nothing. He looked at the face of his opponent and felt very calm.

Evelien said, "Why does he want anything to do with Zupan?"

"He wants something he can't have."

"The pictures?"

"No. More than pictures. Zupan could give him the photographs and Raven might tear them in half. He wants something Zupan took from him. *Somebody.*"

"Next question," she said. "Does it matter?"

"No," Vokkert said again. "We will take care of Raven and then others will understand the fate awaiting them if they try and take us on." He scoffed. "He said I'd know his name. He thinks he's invincible."

"We'll show him he's not."

"Evelien?"

"Yes, darling?"

"You and your girls better not miss."

VOKKERT SAT in his private office and faced three connected wide-screen monitors. On the bright screens, contained in boxes, were the faces of his surviving crew members. Vokkert shared Raven's picture and updated the group on the night's ambush plan.

Not everybody was on board with the effort.

One of his men said, "We need Raven placated, not killed. Get Caesar to bring Zupan back. If all Raven wants is one man, we should deliver instead of wasting more resources."

"Apparently, you're not paying attention, Olaf. Caesar is dead."

"We don't know for sure."

"He's been out of contact too long to still be alive."

"How much money did we waste on him?"

Others joined and echoed Olaf's protests, mostly those opposed to hiring Caesar to begin with. Vokkert let out a sigh as they fired arguments at him and each other. Then he took the lead again.

"Let me remind all of you who is in charge," Vokkert said. The arguing ceased. "If you like breathing you'll also remember you aren't sitting at the head of the table. We've lost a lot because of Raven. I want payback. The ambush happens tonight."

Vokkert ended the session. He sat back and folded his arms. Maybe he had been better off before he organized the gang into one unified unit. Buggers acted like board room execs, not so-called career criminals.

"Do we have to kill him? He's kinda hot."

Evelien Eulen raised an eyebrow at Tanya.

"This isn't a dating profile, Tanya."

"But look at the guy. He could fall on me and I wouldn't complain if he cracked a rib."

"This is serious." *Oh gawd, I sound like Derick now.*

The third woman in the room said, "Turn it off for ten minutes, Tanya."

"Shut up, Kaylee."

"Bitch."

"Slut!"

"Both of you!" Evelien took a deep breath and decided she knew how Derick felt when talking to his crew.

Tanya and Kaylee didn't usually snap at each other, nor did Tanya get excited about a target. Evelien figured if every other member of the *penose* was on edge, why not Tanya and Kaylee, too?

"Are you two done?"

"Yes," said Tanya.

"Go on," said Kaylee.

Evelien continued filling them in on background. As she spoke, Raven's picture remained on her laptop screen. Tanya stared at the picture and wet her lips.

She'd known the two petite blondes most of her life. They'd grown up together and entered the criminal fraternity in college. It was Evelien who suggested they sell drugs instead of finding regular jobs. Peddling narcotics on their college campus had brought in more money than they ever expected. When Evelien met Derick, the other two women joined his group as well.

During their drug-pushing years, Evelien, Tanya, and Kaylee had learned the value of the gun. They had needed to fight competitors and protect themselves. The fastest way to show an opponent you meant business was to stick a nine-millimeter in his face. Nobody underestimated them twice. From hand-to-hand to firearms, Evelien and her girls knew how to rumble. And they'd graduated from street pushers to a sort-of street action squad.

"Why is Derick only using us now?" Kaylee said. She was the most soft-spoken of the trio, her hair short compared to Tanya's long locks.

"I had to convince him," Evelien said. "Or should I say, another plan not working out convinced him, but if he'd used us in the beginning, there would be no reason to use us now."

"Do we know if this Raven fellow has any help?" Kaylee continued. "What about where he's staying?"

"He's alone. No idea where he's staying. We've planned tonight to get him out of any safe house he might have."

"It's fine," Kaylee said. "I've been wanting to try out my new rifle."

"You've had the gun two weeks," Tanya said, "and you haven't tested it yet?"

"No."

"Why?"

Kaylee grinned. "I've been playing with my gunsmith instead."

"Boo, you whore!"

"Jealous?"

"All right," Evelien said. She closed the laptop lid. "We need to get ready. The meet is in four hours. Any other question?"

Tanya said, "Can't we capture this guy so I can have fun, too?"

"Maybe next time," Evelien said.

44

RAVEN WATCHED VOKKERT'S HOUSE FROM DOWN THE STREET. His dash clock read two a.m.; they'd set the meet for three. When a trio of women carrying totes and one a long case exited the house, Raven had no doubt who they were. Evelien Eulen and her girl squad. He hadn't noted the location of the meet because he had no intention of joining them. But the women were leaving without Vokkert or Zupan. They climbed into a minivan with their gear and drove off. As Raven had suspected, the meet was a trap. Well, he'd come to deal with Vokkert one-on-one. Might as well get on with it.

Raven waited ten minutes. Vokkert didn't depart to join them and nobody arrived to keep him company either. Raven drew the SIG P-210 from under his coat, checked the chamber, and gave the suppressor a reassuring twist. He exited the rental and started toward the house.

A sensor on the porch light detected him. The light snapped on. A chime inside suggested the light also triggered an alarm. Raven didn't care. He fired into the knob and deadbolt, then put power behind a kick. Once. Twice. The impacts jolted up his leg. The locks broke apart under the pounding and Raven pushed his way inside. He extended the SIG in both hands.

He ignored the fancy furnishing and decorations. No sign of Vokkert. Raven advanced with caution. The crime boss had turned off the alarm. Was it connected to the cops or a gun crew standing by for such an alert? Raven stayed calm and continued his search of the ground floor, hallway and rooms.

Raven reached the end of the hall and went back to the living room. Vokkert, pistol in hand, swung around a corner on the other side of the room. Raven aimed low and fired once. The nine-mil slug punched through Vokkert's left leg above the knee. With a cry the *penose* boss toppled. Raven ran around couches and chairs to reach the gang boss as he struggled to rise. A bash on the side of the head stunned Vokkert but did not render him unconscious. The blow took him out of the fight, and Raven used the extra seconds to flip Vokkert onto his belly. He secured the crime boss's arms behind him with a zip tie.

Vokkert wailed into the carpet.

"You'll live," Raven snapped. He flipped Vokkert onto his back. The crime boss was bleeding, gasping, and shifting to accommodate his tied hands. Raven stood over him.

"Why are you doing this to me?" Vokkert yelled.

"I want Branko Zupan. Your girlfriend didn't leave with him."

"What have you done to her? Tell me!"

"For all I know, she's at the meet waiting for me. How long do you think she'll stay, Derick?"

"Zupan isn't here, Raven! He hasn't been here for weeks."

"Where do I find him?"

"I don't know! I want him as much as you."

"Why?"

"He disobeyed orders! I told him not to chase a fairy tale and he ignored me."

"You didn't want the pictures yourself?"

"Raven, those pictures are only bringing a world of hurt onto everybody who goes near them. I didn't want Zupan bringing me trouble by default."

"Whoops. Here I am."

"You could have asked me, you know! There was no reason to kill my guys."

Raven scoffed. "It's the only language people like you understand."

"Either that or you're a lunatic."

"You haven't answered my question."

"Okay, okay. I sent somebody to go get Branko but I think he's dead."

"Who?"

"I sent Caesar, the assassin."

"He was in Zagreb?"

"I told him he might find a lead there."

Raven froze. He and Ana had speculated as much; or had only Ana? Raven doubted his recall. He was too focused on Vokkert as the solution to his problem. Now he realized he might be staring at a dead end; the Amsterdam visit a waste of time. Branko Zupan was on the loose with the pictures and planning his next move. He might have made his move already.

Raven tried his last thread of a chance. "You had to have communicated with Zupan in the past. How?"

"Um…phone?"

"Where's your phone?"

Vokkert rolled onto his left side. His cell was secured to his right hip. Raven plucked the phone free and took three steps back. The phone wasn't password protected, and Raven scrolled through the contact list.

No Zupan.

"He isn't here, Derick."

"Look under H for 'headache'."

Raven scrolled up and found the listing.

"He's always been a problem," Vokkert said.

Raven clicked on the name with his thumb and memorized the number. He dropped the phone beside Vokkert.

"You gonna kill me?"

Raven watched Vokkert sweat. A drop trickled down the side of his face to drip onto the carpet.

"It's best you turn over a new leaf, Mr. Vokkert. I don't like Amsterdam. Don't make me come back."

Raven turned and put away his gun as he walked out the door. When Evelien and her squad returned, they could take care of the big boss.

Raven ran back to his car, repeating Zupan's number as he moved. Oscar Morey could trace the location of the cell based on the number. When he was back on the road heading north, he called his old friend.

"You okay, Sam?"

Raven paused before answering but told Oscar the truth.

"You let him live?"

"I lost myself for a while, Oscar. I don't want to compound the mistake. I'm okay now."

"What do you need?"

"Trace on a cell number."

"Give."

Raven repeated the number.

"Got it. Stand by."

Raven kept the phone to his ear and drove. He watched the traffic, keeping to the speed limit. The road signs told him how much further he had to go before the interchange to get back to the city.

He tried to keep his mind from wandering while he waited.

Why are you doing this to me?

An honest question with a complicated answer considering Raven had made a bad call. Yeah, he'd lost himself for a bit, but now he was back on track. Vokkert might have crossed his radar someday. If he didn't follow Raven's advice, there'd be a return engagement in the future. If he had a future after his final meeting with Branko Zupan.

Oscar returned to the phone. "Sorry, Sam. Dead phone."

"What do you mean?"

"I can't ping the number. It's probably been destroyed. Whoever you're trying to trace—"

"Doesn't want anybody to find him."

"Zupan?"

"Yes," Raven said.

Anger flared within him, replaced by disappointment. Raven felt useless and defeated. He'd been playing games while Zupan ran free. He should have paid attention to Ana Gray's hunch. Trying to find Caesar might have been the better play.

"You still there, Sam?"

"Thanks, Oscar, I'll be in touch."

Raven ended the call and dropped the phone on the passenger seat. He gripped the wheel hard with both hands. *Dammit!* What now? Where did he go next? He had nothing. The hunt would start from scratch. And how long until Zupan made use of the compromising pictures? How long before he set off a disturbance in the United States like none had ever seen?

It was late. His energy level had dropped. What he needed was a night's sleep and a clear head when he woke up.

He made the interchange and looked at the lights of Amsterdam ahead.

RAVEN PUSHED OPEN the hotel room door and froze.

A naked woman stood in front of the window. At least she'd left the drapes closed. She faced him with her hands cupped in front of her. She looked nervous. She trembled under his gaze. Her skin was pasty white. Small petite frame, too thin and bony. Her face was bare of make-up. She looked hungry.

Raven shut the door and threw the lock. He saw no need to take out his gun because the woman had nowhere to find one. Instinct won out anyway. He removed the P-210. The woman gasped. Raven checked the bathroom and closet. Nobody else waited. He put the gun away and faced the woman.

"Hi," he said. "Who the hell are you?"

The woman only blinked in reply.

45

THE SHARP STENCH OF CORDITE HUNG IN THE ROOM. BRANKO Zupan put away his pistol. Jasna and Petra stared at him. Milos and Klaus stood waiting for orders. The bodies of Caesar and his woman leaked blood onto the carpet.

Jasna said, "Did you have to kill them inside the house?"

"What's the problem?"

"I'm not cleaning the blood."

"Same," Petra said. She slung her weapon.

Zupan turned to Milos and Klaus and gestured to the bodies. "Go dig a hole and drop them in."

"Where?"

"Anywhere away from here, dammit."

Petra cursed and left the room. Zupan tracked her with a frown. She opened the front door and went outside. Zupan turned to Jasna. She shrugged.

Klaus said, "Got a shovel?"

"Try the garage," Zupan told him. Milos and Klaus departed. Zupan stared at Caesar's body. He might as well have stepped on a cockroach for all the reaction he had to the killing.

He left the bodies, grabbing the envelope of pictures. There were bigger things to think about now. He asked Jasna to join him in the kitchen. He put water in a tea kettle and lit a burner underneath.

"I'm concerned about Petra." He leaned on the counter and folded his arms. "She's going to crack."

"Then we need to move fast. Quit this fooling around."

"Caesar was necessary to deal with."

"Your little performance—"

"Disarmed him. You should thank me. I made one of the toughest killers in the world docile enough to dispose of."

Jasna scoffed. "Toughest this, toughest that. The labels are ridiculous."

"He was like us, Jasna. Same wants and needs. All I did was exploit them."

"Derick will send another."

Zupan shrugged. The kettle whistled. He filled the kettle with tea bags and grabbed a mug from the cupboard. He offered Jasna a cup but she refused. She crossed the kitchen to the back door and went outside.

Petra set her weapon near a rock and sat on the boulder. With her elbows on her knees, she stared at the ocean below the cliff's edge. The cold wind didn't bother her; she was flush with heat after the shooting.

She wanted to scream. The killings strained any remaining ability to block out the violence. She had to find a way out of the dark tunnel in which she found herself.

Footsteps crunched on the dirt behind her. She didn't turn.

"Petra, are you okay?"

"Go away!" Petra shouted. Jasna stopped beside her. "Can't I have ten second alone? *Without* you climbing up my ass?"

"Branko needs to know he can count on you."

"Where else am I going?" Petra said. "Over the cliff?"

"Keep it together a little longer. We'll be done soon. Safe harbor anywhere you want."

"Leave me alone, Jasna."

The older of the two Lovrekovic sisters walked back to the house. Petra remained seated. She hoped her sister was right, or she'd have to find another way out of her life. Going over the cliff seemed like a viable option.

Her sister had never lied to her before. She'd lasted this long. Another few weeks wouldn't be hard. And maybe she'd find another way out in the meantime.

ZUPAN SAT at the dining table. Milos and Klaus had carried out the bodies and stayed outside for their security rounds. Despite their protest, Jasna and Petra had cleaned most of the blood out of the carpet. Zupan had lent a hand to stop their complaining.

Zupan sat in the dining table. He examined the pictures of the US president and his VP paramour and thought of their options. Jasna and Petra cooked dinner in the kitchen. Nobody had done much talking since the killings, and the silence suited Zupan. The quiet gave him space to think.

The best way to tell the Americans he had the pictures was to intercept an employee at the US embassy in London. A greeting, message, and proof would set the ball rolling. Visiting the embassy required an appointment. They'd run the risk of detainment too. Best to find an American out and about. It wouldn't be hard. A day or two of surveillance, follow somebody to lunch...

Zupan sighed. It didn't matter how long the protection lasted. They'd have enough time to change identities and leave their old lives behind. They'd vanish forever.

A new life with a fresh start. He'd never been this close before; he couldn't wait to get started.

The front door opened and closed. Zupan looked up from the table as Klaus stopped in the dining room doorway. Milos was with him and looked worried.

"What is it?" Zupan said.

"I got a call from Amsterdam."

Zupan sat up in the chair. "What now?"

"Vokkert is under attack."

"By whom?"

"Somebody looking for you."

"Interesting."

"Mogensen is dead and this person has blown up one of the warehouses."

"He knows how to get attention," Zupan said.

"What should we do?"

Zupan gathered up the pictures and returned them to the envelope. Jasna announced dinner was ready. Zupan told Klaus they should discuss the situation over dinner.

"It's one man?" Zupan said as they brought the dishes to the dining table.

"Reportedly."

Zupan moved around the table setting the plates out. "I want to find out who he is. I keep thinking of the man I shot in Ireland. Sam Raven. We never confirmed he was dead. If he survived, we'll have to do something. Vokkert isn't equipped to deal with a threat like this."

Jasna yelled for help carrying items to the table.

Within 24 hours Klaus's contact in Amsterdam relayed more information. The man harassing Derick Vokkert identified himself as Sam Raven. Zupan cursed. Raven wasn't dead after all. And Zupan knew what Raven was after. He didn't want the pictures. He wanted revenge for the death of the woman with him in Wexford.

He wanted Jasna and Petra and Milos to go with him to Amsterdam. Klaus would stay at the house with the pictures. Zupan wasn't worried about him taking off with the photos. There was nowhere he could hide if he tried.

Petra listened without comment. Their new life meant nothing if Sam Raven was dogging their trail. They had to deal with him before proceeding with their plans.

But Petra had another thought during the discussion. What if she joined forces with Raven? Could he provide the way out she wanted? She'd have to ensure a clean getaway. It dawned on her the only way to achieve such a goal was to kill her sister and Zupan. It was the only roadblock to her idea. And if she didn't, Raven might pull the trigger for her. She'd have the same result either way. Zupan had reached the point where the world might be better off without him. Maybe she could convince her sister to come along. They had become what they had tried to fight; as evil as the Serbs and mercenaries who terrorized Croatia. What Petra wanted more than anything was a chance at redemption.

The only question was how to make contact with Raven.

Jasna suggested the answer. She had the idea of sending Petra ahead to trap the American.

"How?" Petra asked.

"You know how. He's a man."

Petra didn't like the idea but had to admit it solved her problem.

Zupan made the travel plans. They'd leave the next day on an afternoon flight. Chartered, of course. Their baggage would contain killing tools.

46

RAVEN SAID, "YOU GOING TO SAY ANYTHING OR STAND THERE like a shivering wet cat?"

"Um--"

"Wait. I've seen you before. You were in a car. In Ireland."

"I can—"

"Get your clothes on. Tell my why you're here and when you're done talking, I might let you live. I've only shot a nude woman once and would rather pass on a second time."

The woman moved fast and breathed hard as she grabbed for the pile of clothes at her feet. As she pulled on her panties and jeans, she talked fast.

"Yes, I am with Zupan. They're in the lobby waiting for me." She zipped the jeans and grabbed her bra and T-shirt. "I'm the bait." Petra spoke with more confidence now. "They made me come up here. I was supposed to—"

"Seduce me?" Raven tried not to laugh. Another time and place, maybe. After she ate and gained thirty pounds.

"Distract you. We'll have a visitor in a minute."

Raven shifted to a spot between the bed and wall, which put him out of direct line with the door.

"And you're telling me because—"

"I want your help." She shoved her arms through the T-shirt.

"Sure."

"I mean it." She stood with her arms at her sides. "My sister and Zupan are out of control. I've had enough. I want out. I'll tell you everything you want. The pictures are in Wales. But you have to take me away from them."

"You want me to kill your sister and Zupan, too?"

"The thought had occurred to me. Yes."

The door crashed open with a thud against the opposite wall. Petra screamed. Raven pivoted with the P-210 extended. Milos entered and said, "Where is he?" Petra shook her head.

Raven said, "Here, ass," and shot Milos in the head. Blood and bits of skull splattered on the wall. The gunman fell in a heap. Raven turned back to Petra.

"You'll get worse if you're lying to me, little girl."

"My name is Petra."

"I suggest we get going."

He and Petra ran out of the room. He was leaving behind his clothes and gear but there was no time to pack. He needed a new place to hide and a way to Wales and fast.

Raven pushed Petra ahead as they traveled down the stairwell to the lobby.

"Where are Jasna and Zupan?"

"If not in the lobby waiting, they'll be somewhere else. I'm not sure."

They passed another floor. Raven's mind raced. Where to go, who to call. The answer came fast. The obvious answer. But he needed to get them both away from the hotel first.

They avoided the lobby and exited into the parking garage. Raven kept Petra ahead of him. They stayed close to parked cars on their left and moved at a quick pace. Raven's rental waited at the end of the row. Their footsteps echoed on the concrete. The garage was cold. Raven's eyes darted back and forth searching for threats.

He watched Petra, too. He didn't want to let her get too far away. Then footsteps not their own shuffled and steel bumped metal and Raven yelled, "Down!" He pushed Petra to the floor and landed on top as two shots cracked across the aisle. The rounds came from his right and punched through a car's back window. More shuffling footsteps. Raven scanned for a target; saw none. He rolled off Petra and told her to run for his car. As she rose, he fired at movement behind a support pillar. The nine-mil slug whined off the concrete. Zupan eased around the back of a car. Raven fired twice. Zupan ducked as one shot hit the car and the other sparked off the corner of the wall behind him.

Petra yelled for Raven. She squatted beside the rental. Raven fired a third shot where Zupan had been. He ran for the rental and replaced the partially spent magazine with a full one, pocketing the other. Reaching the rental, he used the key remote to unlock the doors. He and Petra piled in and the engine rumbled to life.

"Stay down!" Raven reversed, spun the wheel, and stepped hard on the accelerator. He glanced in the rearview mirror. Jasna and Zupan took aim and fired. Two shots smacked into the back glass; one passed through to rip into the center of the dash.

Raven turned right. He continued along the ramp to the exit and screeched onto the street. He pressed the gas to speed up. Petra rose and rested against the passenger backrest.

"Are you hurt?" he asked.

"No."

"What will they do now?"

"They might chase us."

"Or?"

"If they figure out what I've done they'll go back to Wales."

"Uh-huh."

Raven made a few sharp turns, finally picked up a motorway. He stayed in the right lane and dialed a number on his cell. First call went to voicemail; he called again and Damien, Ana's man in the city, answered.

"Who is this?"

"Raven."

"Do you know what time it is?"

"I'm burned and I need a place to hide right now."

"Are you kidding me?"

"No," Raven said. "Now."

"All right, all right." He gave Raven an address and directions. As he drove, Raven realized he was going the wrong way. Damien continued, "No cars allowed in this part of the city. You'll need to park and walk."

"Fine."

"I'll meet you there. Anything else?"

"More when I see you."

Raven hung up and set the phone in the center console. Wind whistled through the hole in the back window.

Petra said, "Who did you call?"

"Never mind."

"You don't trust me."

"Are you surprised?" He grinned at her. "You're either telling the truth or leading me to the showdown I've been waiting for."

"I'm not lying. I could have let Milos kill you."

"Who?"

"The man you shot in your room."

"Oh. Him. Well, we'll see won't we."

Raven took the next exit and drove back onto the motorway going the opposite direction. Fifteen minutes and a walk to Damien's hideout. He kept checking behind him for tails. And he kept glancing at the woman beside him. He wasn't buying her damsel act yet.

47

ZUPAN AND JASNA DROVE IN CIRCLES FOR A FEW BLOCKS BUT saw no sign of Raven's car. Zupan pulled over. He left the engine running and turned to Jasna.

"What the hell is she doing?"

"She got soft, she told him everything."

"And she wants him to get her away from us?"

"You were right, Branko."

"I didn't want to be."

"I know." ₁

"What do we do?" Zupan said.

"She's betrayed us. I will kill her myself, not you. Do you understand, Branko?"

Zupan said he understood. He put the car in gear and drove away.

THE NARROW ENTRYWAY looked like a good place for an ambush.

Raven kept the P-210 close to his right leg as he ascended

the steps behind Petra. They were entering the typical Amsterdam dwelling. Narrow and tall. As they went up the steps, he kept bumping his left shoulder on the wall. Finally, they stopped at the fourth-floor landing. The brown door before them had "401" on the front. Raven knocked. He slipped his right index finger onto the SIG-Sauer's trigger.

The deadbolt snapped back and Damien opened the door.

"Ana says you're gonna owe her for this one."

"Her or you?"

Damien scoffed. "Me."

"Say so. Let us in."

"You didn't say you had a guest."

I've heard that before. "I have a guest," Raven said.

Damien cursed and allowed them inside. He locked the door. Raven said, "How much?"

"How long you staying?"

"Only until we can get out of here. Day or two."

"Fine." Damien showed them around. It was a small place. It looked to Raven like an enlarged janitor's closet with plumbing added.

"I trust you weren't followed?" Damien said.

"No, we weren't."

"There's food and drinks, and hot water. What else? You need more hardware?"

Raven handed the other man a slip of paper from his shirt pocket. Damien examined the list.

"I'll get on this."

"Bill me."

"No. You pay before you leave. I'm not taking the chance of you not surviving the week."

Damien left and Raven explored the very clean kitchen. Petra dropped on a couch and crossed her legs and arms.

"What did you ask him for?"

Raven said, "Ammo, guns and clothes." He exited the

kitchen and took a chair across from her. A small coffee table occupied the space between them.

"What are we going to do?" she said.

"You get some rest. I'll stay awake and keep watch."

"You really don't trust me, do you?"

"No."

"You saw me. I have no weapons."

"Plenty of knives in the kitchen."

"Raven, please."

"It's too soon, Petra. And the last time I took in a broken wing it didn't go well. Your man saw to that."

"Branko is not *my* man."

"You people. You killed her."

"It wasn't my decision."

"You didn't want to, is that it?"

"I've had no choice but to follow them, Raven. Jasna is my sister. Branko saved our lives once."

"Uh-huh."

"But the last few years have been terrible. I can't take it anymore."

"You said so already. You're looking for a life boat."

She lowered her eyes. "I guess, yeah. You aren't going to help me, are you?"

"What am I supposed to do, Petra? Where are you going to go when it's over?"

She shrugged. "I don't know. My whole life, Raven. Ever since—"

"The war, I get it. War is hell and all that. Tell me about it."

"Don't mock me."

"You have to look at the situation from my perspective."

"I'm the enemy."

"I've torn through this city to get to your man."

"He's not my—"

"And suddenly you show up. Nice and convenient. You

even sacrificed one of your guys. Or something. Do you understand why I don't trust you, or do I have to explain it like you're a two-year-old?"

She glared at him.

"Stop it, Petra. Here'd what I want. Take me to Zupan and your sister. I'll do my thing. Then I will destroy the photographs and go away. What you do next doesn't matter to me. You're on your own."

"Okay."

"And Petra?"

"What?"

"You try anything, I'll cut off your head and shit down your neck."

Color drained from her face. She whispered, "All right."

"I suggest you use the bedroom upstairs. Stay there till I come get you."

She didn't reply. In a hurry she left the couch and went up the stairs. Raven waited. When he heard the door close, he finally let out a sigh and tried to relax.

He should never have set foot in Barcelona. Had he stayed at home, in Stockholm, on his houseboat, he never would have crossed paths with Megan. She may or may not have survived her initial clash, but he'd be none the wiser. If he didn't know, he couldn't care.

But he was in Amsterdam because he *did* care. He wished he didn't. He wasn't a monster. He did what he did because it was important. Important for *something* though he wasn't sure how quite to put it into words. But he knew it was true.

Petra *seemed* genuine. He didn't think she was lying but he had to stay cold. He had no more room for any emotions. Not now. Maybe later when the enemy no longer posed a threat. If Petra died, it was her own fault. He had a task to complete and intended to do so no matter what.

It was a lousy way of life. He wanted out too. As he felt

for the locket under his shirt, he realized he knew something Petra didn't. There might not *be* a way out. He had none and it was silly to think otherwise. The only way out was a bullet in the back--someday. He had to make the best of what life gave him in the meantime.

If Petra was lucky, she'd be more fortunate than he.

———————————

PETRA LAY on the bed and wondered if she should have leaped off the cliff when she had the chance.

Raven was no different than those from which she was trying to escape.

No way back now, she knew. Branko and Jasna would treat her like any other traitor. She'd seen their reactions too many times over the years to doubt one second what her fate might be if they caught her. No hesitation. She was doomed if Raven failed.

She rolled onto her side, fully dressed on top of the comforter. There was no reason to get undressed and under the covers. At least the bed was comfortable. She had to think the best. She'd get away. The rest of her life was hers to create in any way she wanted.

She hoped.

Petra finally dozed off. Raven was right about one thing. She'd need rest for the coming journey.

48

DAMIEN CAME THROUGH WITH NINE-MIL AMMO FOR RAVEN'S
pistol and the "something heavier" he'd asked for too. The
M4A1 carbine suited Raven fine, and the AKS-74U for Petra
fit her small hands too. Damien included six spare mags and
ammo for each weapon. The clothes he bought for Petra
were a little too big but suitable; Raven was a much easier fit.

"What about passports?" Damien asked. "How are you
getting into the UK?"

The lack of proper passports for either of them had
dawned on Raven after Petra went to bed. A decision still
eluded him when he finally let himself fall asleep.

"We will need to land somewhere other than an airport,"
he said. He also provided no further details. Petra's descrip-
tion of the open country around the safe house meant a
landing was possible. But his usual source of airborne transportation wouldn't cooperate with such a plan. He'd have to
call and wait for another pilot, with a different type of plane,
for entry into the UK. It meant waiting a bit longer, but
Damien promised to add the extra time to the bill. Raven
told him he was all heart.

Within 48 hours Raven had his pilot. A British mercenary named Goddin knew the area they were flying into and agreed to the flight. With the gear packed, and Raven and Petra as prepared as time allowed, they set off in Goddin's Piper Cherokee.

ZUPAN AND JASNA returned to the safe house where Klaus waited with the pictures. The three began preparing for the arrival of Raven and Petra.

The space around the house contained small rocks, scattered boulders, and trees. It was difficult to determine where Raven might attack from, so they spread the coverage between the three of them. On the second night of their watch, Zupan and Jasna walked the house perimeter together.

"Like the old days," Zupan said.

"Too much like the old days," Jasna said. "She could have tricked him, you know. Pretended to want help while meaning to lead him to us."

"And Milos? Was he a sacrifice?"

Jasna had no answer.

"Why wait?" Zupan continued. "She could have handed him over in Amsterdam, assuming she didn't mean for Milos to die. But she left with Raven. Don't tell me *you're* getting soft, too?"

Jasna let chirping crickets and the distant ocean crash fill her lack of response.

"Answer me, Jasna."

She said, "No."

"She's turned on us, Jasna. You know what has to happen to traitors. You said so yourself."

"I know, but—"

"If you hesitate, I will shoot her."

"I know."

"Then it will be only you and me like we always wanted."

"Always," she said, but she didn't look at him and her eyes filled with tears. She felt the drops trickle down her cheeks. In the dark, Zupan had no idea. He wasn't looking at her either. Jasna took a deep breath and felt thankful she didn't sob.

They'd dealt with traitors many times in the past. But she never thought she'd turn a gun on her own sister.

Petra, how could you...

THE BRIT PILOT, Goddin, landed his Piper in a field at noon the next day.

High noon, Raven thought. *Appropriate.*

Goddin helped Raven unload the plane. Raven said, "Give us a couple of hours. If we don't come back, get out of here."

"Sure you don't want help?" the pilot said.

"If we make it back, we'll need all kinds of help. But for now, we'll manage."

Raven took a moment to lock and load the M4A1 and Petra cocked her AKS. She took the lead and Raven followed. They crested a low rise. The ocean thrashed a mile to the right. The mission had begun at the ocean's edge in Spain and was ending at the ocean's edge in Wales. Raven found peace in the juxtaposition. One way or another, the ocean horizon would lead to something better, as Megan had believed, in this life or the next.

Raven and Petra took cover behind a patch of overgrown bushes. The safe house sat 50 yards ahead. The trees and boulders looked like good cover, but Raven knew otherwise. Small cover wasn't any better than no cover. But he didn't see much choice. He had to maximize what he had available. Waiting for the sun to go down might be the better option. Had he a full kit, he'd have indeed waited. He didn't have the luxury this time. Their biggest advantage was the sun at their backs, and it was almost as good as the cover of night.

"What are they doing inside?" Raven asked Petra.

"It's Jasna, Branko, and Milos. They'll cover three sides and two will overlap the fourth. It's been a few days so they're tired. They'll have been sleeping in shifts."

"Weapons?"

"Small arms. Limited ammo. We weren't planning for an attack and didn't mean to stay here this long."

Another point in Raven's favor.

He wished he had a few grenades to shake the foundation. Glancing to his right, he found a rock the size of his palm. Almost as good if he could put it through a window. They'd think it was a grenade and react accordingly. It might buy him an extra two or three seconds.

Raven stuffed the rock in a pocket. "Come on."

He took the lead now. Raven rose and circled around the bushes, Petra behind him and to the left. He dashed to a tree. Petra dropped flat across from him. He told her to stay and open fire as soon as he tossed the rock. She nodded.

Raven moved forward, rock in hand, and stood as he flung. He was aiming at one of the side windows. He hit the ground and Petra's AKS-74U popped twice behind him. The rock crashed through the window. Somebody inside yelled. Barrels poked out the windows and return fire blasted back. Raven sighted with the M4A1 and fired. More glass shattered; Raven's 5.56mm slugs punched holes in the side of the house. Return salvos smacked the trees around him.

Petra triggered another string of fire. Raven rolled right and ran closer to the house. He wanted to get inside. A burst kicked up dirt near him. He rolled away again. A boulder covered him now. Fifteen yards to go. If he made it around the corner he'd be on the front porch. A full-auto burst went off, but none of the rounds came near him. He frowned. Somebody screamed inside. The shooting stopped and a woman began yelling in a language he didn't understand.

The shouting inside stopped. Petra yelled, "Raven, hold your fire! My sister is coming out!"

49

THE WINDOW SHATTERED AND JASNA WATCHED AN OBJECT FLY into the house. "Grenade!"

The rock bounced off the back of the couch.

"No!" Zupan shouted. "They're on the left!"

Jasna, Zupan, and Milos crawled across the carpet. The shooting started. Bullets punched through the windows and wall. Zupan smashed a window and stuck the barrel of his rifle out. Taking a quick peek, careful not to raise his head too high, he pulled the trigger. His rifle cracked with each single shot. Jasna and Milos lined up on his right and left.

With the sun in their face, it was hard to see the targets. Jasna squinted and peered down the length of her rifle. She couldn't see Petra. Slugs smacked through the wall over her head. Bits of sheetrock landed in her hair.

When Raven ran to get closer, Zupan held back the trigger for a full-auto burst. The salvo stitched a line a few feet in front of Raven and the American moved out of the way.

Jasna finally spotted Petra. Behind a rock. Aiming at the house. But aiming high. Jasna sighted on her sister's head and took up slack on the trigger, but then released the pressure. She dropped below the window sill and removed her finger from the fire control.

No.

She could not kill the only flesh-and-blood she had left in the world.

She looked at Zupan as he took aim. Milos was doing the same. Jasna raised her rifle at the two men. Her first full-auto burst chopped Milos down and splashed blood on the wall beside him. Zupan turned startled eyes on her. She raised the rifle stock over her head, and Zupan screamed. She hammered the buttstock into his face. He fell back, unconscious.

Jasna moved away from the windows and yelled to Petra in their native language. She waited. The shooting outside ceased. Petra yelled to Raven. Jasna shouted, "Coming out now!" in English and slung her rifle. She grabbed Zupan under each arm and started dragging him toward the front door.

Raven reached the porch. Jasna opened the front door. He aimed his M4 at her but lowered the weapon when he saw she had no weapon in hand. She dragged Branko Zupan onto the steps. Zupan started moaning.

"Don't shoot, Raven," Jasna said. Raven stepped back. Petra ran to them.

"What are you doing?" Petra said to her sister.

"I give up." Jasna dragged Zupan off the steps and dropped him in the dirt. He moaned and shifted.

Jasna faced Raven. He held the M4 down but left his finger on the trigger.

"He's all yours," Jasna said.

"Really."

"I can't hurt my sister. She's all I have."

Petra put a hand to her mouth.

"It's too bad," Raven said, "you weren't so charitable to those who died in pursuit of those pictures."

"I can't bring those people back. Everything was Branko's idea. The pictures are in the house."

"Better hand them over."

Jasna ran into the house. Raven watched Zupan try and get up. He failed and curled as he moaned again. The blow to his face looked painful indeed, the red welt extended from his left eye to the corner of his mouth.

Petra said, "I didn't expect this."

"Neither did I," he told her.

Jasna returned and tossed the envelope at Raven's feet.

"Do whatever you want with them."

"What do you want in return?"

"We have a van. Let me and Petra go. Zupan is yours."

Kill them all.

Raven winced at the thought. He clenched his teeth.

Do it fast while you have the chance.

Kill them. Now!

Raven backed up further. "Get out of here. If I ever see you two again, I promise it won't end well."

Petra and Jasna set their weapons down. Petra ran with Jasna to the garage side where the car waited. Doors opened and closed. The engine started. Raven watched the van back up and turn onto the dirt road. The van with the Lovrekovic sisters inside sped away.

Idiot.

I'm not a monster.

Jasna was right. She couldn't bring back the victims and neither can I. The killing can't go on forever.

Zupan finally pushed to his feet. He managed to get halfway when Raven snapped out of his thoughts. He shoved Zupan back down with a foot.

"Where you going, bub?"

Zupan muttered gibberish. Raven set down the M4A1 and took out the SIG P-210. He thumbed back the hammer. Kneeling beside Zupan, Raven grabbed a handful of Zupan's hair and lifted him up till their eyes met. Raven put the SIG against Zupan's forehead.

"You missed me in Ireland," Raven said.

"No," Zupan managed.

"Sucks, don't it?"

Raven applied pressure to the trigger, easing it back, counting one, two, three—

The gun cracked between three and four. The nine-mil slug bored through Zupan's head. The force of the blast jerked his head from Raven's grasp.

Raven stood and collected the envelope from the ground. He checked the contents. Jasna had not pulled a fast one. He entered the house, searching each room. Nobody hiding. In the kitchen, he looked for matches and found a box in a drawer. He put the pictures in a pot and set the pot on the stove. Lighting several matches, he held the flame to the corners of the pictures. The kitchen filled with smoke as the pictures began to burn. Raven took the pot out to the porch and set it down. He watched the flame devour the pictures.

He'd pass the word along to his contacts at CIA and let them know he'd destroyed the pictures. Whether they believed him or not he didn't care.

Within fifteen minutes the flame reduced the pictures to ash. He left them in the pot and picked up the M4A1. It was a long hike back to Goddin and the Piper Cherokee, but the Brit was waiting when Raven returned.

"There were two of you," Goddin said.

"She went her own way."

"Climb in."

Raven set the carbine in the rear seat and joined Goddin inside. The pilot started the engine and the propeller spun to life. Raven sat and stared out the window in a daze. He felt no sense of achievement. He had avenged Megan, but she was still gone, and he remained alone.

Now he had to figure out what to do next. For the first time in his life, he had no idea.

50

GODDIN'S CONNECTIONS IN LONDON FIXED RAVEN WITH A new passport and he used it to leave the UK and fly to Barcelona. He drove from the airport to Ana Gray's house.

Her new butler answered the door. "She's waiting for you, sir."

Raven followed the butler to the upper floor where Ana sat on the balcony. She stood and smiled at him. The butler departed. She wore her usual outfit and diamond necklace.

"I knew you'd come back," she said.

"Thanks for everything you did, Ana. I got him."

"The pictures?"

"Up in smoke."

"You don't look pleased, though."

"Someday I'll be able to explain why. I'm not sure myself right now."

"Wait here. I have something for you. Please sit. I'll have the butler bring you a drink."

"Water is fine."

She brushed past him on her way inside. Raven sat. A plane flew overhead. He watched the jet descend to the airport. He didn't want to fly on any more planes. He wanted to be done with travel in general. He wanted to end his entire crusade. It didn't escape him that he was back in Barcelona in the same mental state as when he first arrived. Tired. Worn out. And the deaths of Sebastian and Megan made him want out more than before.

What he needed was a long rest and time for soul searching. There was a lot to come to terms with. He wanted as much time as it took to sort the demons in his head.

The butler arrived with his ice water. A lemon wedge sat on the rim of the glass. He squeezed the lemon into the water and drank down half. He hadn't realized he was so thirsty.

Ana returned and he stood as she reached the table. She held an ornate wooden box. Raven's heart sank. She set the box on the table.

"My people got her body out of Ireland," Ana said. "I had her cremated."

Raven lifted the lid. Inside sat a plastic bag full of gray ash. The sum total of one's life. A few pounds of ash in a box. Tomorrow it would be as if Megan had never existed.

But he'd never forget her.

"I figure you know what to do?" she said.

"Yes," Raven replied. He lowered the lid.

ONE BEACH WAS as good as another; one ocean view identical to the rest.

Raven drove his rental to Sebastian's old place and parked in the public lot. The businesses along the street next to the bar looked busy as he followed the sidewalk. He paused at the bar. Somebody had removed the signs and put a "For Lease" ad in the front window.

Raven continued forward. He walked with purpose, a

man with a task, and if anybody noticed he paid no attention. Once at the beach, he climbed a hill and walked some more. He let the waves overpower his thoughts. He didn't want to think anymore. All he wanted was peace and quiet.

He stopped at a jagged cliff and looked at the rocks thirty feet below. Waves crashed against them, coating the rocks with a perpetual sheen of foamy salt water. The air smelled fresh and he found the sensation invigorating. Megan had always found peace and hope when staring at the ocean's horizon; he did too. Everything would be all right in its own time. He didn't plan to rush his healing process.

Raven knelt, opened the box, and cut the bag open with a pocket knife. Holding the ashes carefully in both hands, he stepped to the edge.

"I'm sorry you had such a hard time," he said. He had to speak loudly to hear himself over the surf. "I hope now you can rest."

He turned over the bag and dumped Megan's remains onto the rocks below. The falling dust left a lingering cloud. Some of the dust stuck to his clothes. Raven shook the bag empty and looked down again. The ashes coated the rocks. He stayed and watched until the ocean washed away the last remnants of Megan, then lifted his head to the horizon.

RAVEN FOUND no reason to leave right away. He returned to his hotel. He wanted solitude, but after a late dinner he found sleep impossible. It was after midnight when he said the hell with it, rose and dressed again, and went for a walk.

The street was quiet but activity in a few bars remained strong. He paused in front of one bar. He watched the young people inside enjoying their night. He wished he was one of them instead of who he really was.

He walked on. The locket under his shirt felt heavy. He hoped the ghosts would understand and leave him alone for a while.

Another block. He passed more late partiers who didn't give him a second glance. Another block. Businesses closed; alleys dark; street lamps hummed as their light filled the street. As always, Raven carried a weapon. The suppressor-fitted SIG P-210 rose under his jacket. Someday he'd be able to go without a gun.

A woman screamed.

He stopped, senses alert.

"Let go of me! No!"

His eyes darted across the street. He scanned empty alleys and stopped when motion in one finally caught his attention. Two people, a female struggling against the grasp of a larger male.

"Let me go!" the woman shouted.

The slap following the cry sounded like a rifle shot.

Raven didn't hesitate. He grabbed for his gun and ran to the alley.

A LOOK AT: NO NAME ON MY GRAVE: A SAM RAVEN THRILLER

BY BRIAN DRAKE

Sam Raven Races Against Time to Stop a Takeover of the United States!

They're hiding in plain sight, all over the USA. Enemies planted by a mastermind with world domination in mind. First, he needs to take the United States off the world's stage and insert selected puppets. Violent attacks on American citizens show no mercy leaving thousands dead, and many more injured.

Sam Raven learns of the plot from somebody involved, somebody trying to escape once the horror of the conspiracy became reality, and gathers his motley crew of misfit Raiders to take the fight straight to the enemy.

The enemy runs deep, and resources Raven once counted on are now against him. But they forgot Raven is most dangerous when he's alone.

AVAILABLE AUGUST 2025

ABOUT THE AUTHOR

A twenty-five year veteran of radio and television broadcasting, Brian Drake has spent his career in San Francisco where he's filled writing, producing, and reporting duties with stations such as KPIX-TV, KCBS, KQED, among many others. Currently carrying out sports and traffic reporting duties for Bloomberg 960, Brian Drake spends time between reports and carefully guarded morning and evening hours cranking out action/adventure tales.

A love of reading when he was younger inspired him to create his own stories, and he sold his first short story, "The Desperate Minutes," to an obscure webzine when he was 25 (more years ago than he cares to remember, so don't ask).

Brian Drake lives in California with his wife and two cats, and when he's not writing he is usually blasting along the back roads in his Corvette with his wife telling him not to drive so fast, but the engine is so loud he usually can't hear her.

briandrakebooks.com